OF THE
GRIZZLY

THE YEAR
OF THE
GRIZZLY

★ ★ ★

BROCK & BODIE THOENE

BETHANY HOUSE PUBLISHERS
MINNEAPOLIS, MINNESOTA 55438

Cover by Dan Thornberg,
Bethany House Publishers staff artist.

Copyright © 1992
Brock and Bodie Thoene
All Rights Reserved

Published by Bethany House Publishers
A Ministry of Bethany Fellowship, Inc.
6820 Auto Club Road, Minneapolis, Minnesota 55438

Printed in the United States of America

Library of Congress Cataloging-in-Publication Data

Thoene, Brock, 1952–
   The year of the grizzly / Brock & Bodie Thoene.
      p. cm. — (Saga of the Sierras)

   1. California—History—1846–1850—Fiction.
I. Thoene, Bodie, 1951–   . II. Title.
III. Series: Thoene, Brock, 1952–   Saga of the Sierras.
PS3570.H463Y35 1992
813'.54—dc20   92–24827
ISBN 1–55661–167–6   CIP

This book is
for Luke . . .

Books by Brock and Bodie Thoene

The Zion Covenant

Vienna Prelude
Prague Counterpoint
Munich Signature
Jerusalem Interlude
Danzig Passage
Warsaw Requiem

The Zion Chronicles

The Gates of Zion
A Daughter of Zion
The Return to Zion
A Light in Zion
The Key to Zion

The Shiloh Legacy

In My Father's House
A Thousand Shall Fall
Say to This Mountain

Saga of the Sierras

The Man From Shadow Ridge
Riders of the Silver Rim
Gold Rush Prodigal
Sequoia Scout
Cannons of the Comstock
The Year of the Grizzly
Shooting Star

Non-Fiction

Protecting Your Income and Your Family's Future
Writer to Writer

BROCK AND BODIE THOENE have combined their skills to become a prolific writing team. Bodie's award-winning writing of THE ZION CHRONICLES and THE ZION COVENANT series is supported by Brock's careful research and development. Co-authors of SAGA OF THE SIERRAS, this husband and wife team has spent years researching the history and the drama of the Old West.

Their work has been acclaimed by men such as John Wayne and Louis L'Amour. With their children, Brock and Bodie live in the Sierras, giving firsthand authenticity to settings and descriptions in this frontier series.

CHAPTER 1

The clanging of the church bells in the twin towers at Mission Santa Barbara rolled lazily over the canyons and hillsides. As the deep-pitched cast-iron voices announced the hour of noon, Will Reed looked up from the flank of the calf he had roped and wiped a buckskin-gloved hand across his sweaty forehead.

He pushed the stringy curls of his dark auburn hair up out of his eyes and gestured for his fourteen-year-old son to hurry up with the branding iron. "Vamos, Peter! Just this one more and we can break for mealtime."

"Coming, Father," the thin, serious youth replied. Peter removed the glowing brand depicting the leaning *R* of the Reed family from the blazing coals of oak. The application of the hot iron sizzled on the hide and brought a sharp bleat of complaint from the calf.

After its ears were notched in a pattern to indicate the year 1846, the red calf was allowed to scamper out of the corral and rejoin the rest of the herd. "Bueno!" shouted the short, round-bellied man who opened and shut the corral gate. "That makes a dozen so far. Young Pedro has the makings of a real vaquero."

"Paco," Peter laughed at the heavyset Mission Indian, "you've said the same thing every roundup since

9

I was five and using my reata to catch Mother's geese. When will I *be* a real vaquero?"

Clearing his throat at the question, Peter's father scowled. "Be careful what you wish for," he said. "The other branding teams will do twenty calves to our twelve, and the roundup lasts for weeks."

"And I would be with them if you and Mother did not make me study geometry and practice writing letters!" complained the boy.

Will swatted the dust from his leather chaparejos with a swipe of the stiff-brimmed hat. "What can we do with such a maverick?" he asked Paco, grinning. "His grandfather is a university educated engineer, but all this whelp can think about is horses and cows!"

Paco shook his head in mock despair. "It must be the other side of his nature coming out," he suggested. "His father, it is said, came across the wilderness from America, and put the Spanish caballeros to shame with his riding and roping. And his ojos verdes, his green eyes! They say he was muy enamorado, a great lover, to win the hand of the flower of California, Francesca Rivera y Cruz."

"Enough!" Will shot back. "It is already too hot for such windy tales. Besides, they will have heard the bells at home and dinner will be waiting. Come on!"

He led the way to where his steel-gray horse stamped and fretted in the shade of the tamarack trees next to Peter's buckskin and Paco's mule. "What is disturbing the horses?" Peter began; then another peal of church bells interrupted him. "What can that be? Is it a fire?"

His father shushed him to silence, and the three men listened to the discordant jangling—not the

clear tones of the single bell, but a confused and un-
certain sound, as if a pile of scrap metal were being
dropped onto stone pavement. Underneath it all, a
muted rumbling grew, like the passage of a distant
stampede.

"It's an earthquake!" shouted Will. "Get away from
the horses!" A sharp, convulsive twist in the ground
beneath him knocked him off his feet. It tossed his son
and Paco into the plunging and rearing mounts, and
the horses scattered.

A sickening corkscrew motion, like a square-rigged
ship facing a quartering sea, followed the initial shock.
Across the plain, Will could see the waves of tremors
rolling like ocean swells.

Paco tried to stand just as another crest passed,
and he was flung outstretched on the ground. "How
long till it quits rolling?" called Peter from where he
hugged a tamarack's trunk. "Quién sabe? Who
knows?" the Indian replied. "The hinges of the earth
are turning, and El Diablo, the devil, is riding out of
the underworld."

———

Don Pedro Rivera y Cruz reached across the heavy
oak plank table toward the clay jar of olives. The jar,
as if possessed with a mind of its own, edged away from
his fingers. "What mischief is this?" Don Pedro muttered to his daughter, who was tasting a kettle of sim-
mering bean and barley stew. Then the shockwave hit,
and the earthenware pot rolled off the table and broke
on the floor. "Earthquake!" he shouted.

Above the hornillo, the brick oven, a crack appeared
in the plaster of the whitewashed adobe. As Francesca

stared in amazement, a spider web of lines branched and forked, like a chain of lightning spreading up the wall.

When the rippling net of cracks reached the top of the wall, it exploded in a cloud of plaster dust that showered down on the dark-haired woman. Another tremor hit, flinging her sharply against the edge of the oak table, knocking out her breath and throwing her to the ground. The hornillo shattered, filling the air with smoke and swirling soot and littering the dirt floor with hot coals. Francesca slapped at the smoldering embers that rolled onto her long skirt.

The crack in the wall widened, and globs of mortar fell from the seams of the adobe blocks. The beams of the roof creaked and groaned, and the heavy brick wall leaned inward, threatening to collapse at any moment.

Don Pedro, somehow still on his feet, crossed the small room with a leap and yanked his daughter out of the wreckage of the stove and flung her toward the doorway. She landed half in and half out of the opening, just as the wall split apart with a crack like the noise of a rifle shot, and the adobe blocks began to fall.

The ranchero had no chance to escape. He lunged for the floor and rolled under the stout wooden table. Fragments of heavy clay slabs rained down, and a roaring sound seemed to come from the earth underneath the cookhouse as the roof collapsed into the interior of the building.

Francesca's roll through the doorway was accelerated by another spasm of the earth. She tumbled over and over in the yard between the tall wood frame house and the adobe kitchen.

When at last the ground stopped spinning, Francesca was facing away from the cookhouse. "Father," she called as she stood slowly, fighting the dizziness, "are you all right?" Turning toward the block building, she gave a scream and tottered forward: the structure had completely shattered and fallen into a shapeless mass of rubble. The roof beams protruded from the wreckage like the ribs of a whale carcass.

"Father!" she screamed again, and fell to trying to shift the great blocks of clay from where the entry had been only moments before. Francesca strained to lift a single brick free of the pile and found that she could not; the ruins seemed to have locked together again into a solid mass.

Even when she found a single wooden post that would reluctantly move when she pulled with all her strength, she was forced to stop when another heap of blocks tumbled into the newly made opening. With an anguished cry, Francesca clawed at the fragments of bricks, tossing them aside. Her nails tore and bled in her frenzied struggle to uncover her father. She called his name again and again, but received no answer.

Simona, the cook, and her husband Luis came running out of the house. "Help me!" Francesca pleaded. "Father is buried underneath and I cannot free him!"

Luis looked at the mound of adobe before glancing at Simona. He shook his head sadly.

"No!" Francesca yelled, denying the dreadful suggestion in the unspoken thought. She pounded her fists on the unrelenting bricks. "No! Father! Father!"

———

The turn of the earth's hinges brought rockslides

and avalanches to the hills around Santa Barbara. The peaks rimming the coastal plain sprouted spirals of dust, as if the mountains had broken into a hundred fires.

Will suddenly thought of Francesca and their house. How well had it withstood the quake? His concern multiplied when he recalled his insistence that their new casa be built in the wood-frame manner of his upbringing, rather than the adobe construction of California.

The horses and the mule and the herd of cattle had run from the terror of the tremors. Will could not locate his mount. The only animal of any kind still in sight was one lone steer.

The rangy, rust-colored Chihuahua longhorn shook his head angrily. The four-foot spread of curved and deadly spikes tossed from side to side.

When the quake struck, the herd of cows had stampeded in all directions, except for the single beast that pawed the ground like a fighting bull. Angered at the unexpected movement of the earth, the two-legged man creatures became the target of blame.

The powerful animal lunged at Paco, who fled to the safety of the tamarack tree beside Peter. Together they climbed its spindly branches. There was barely room above the height of the steer's head for both to cling to the narrowing trunk. The steer's horns clashed against the tree, and he gave a bellow of challenge for them to come down and fight.

The crash of the heavy-headed beast against the slender tree was like the force of another earthquake to the man and the boy. A few more such blows, and they would fall beneath his hooves.

Will slapped his hand against his chaps to attract

the animal's attention. He did not have time for this disturbance right now. At another moment the predicament might have seemed humorous, but not when he so desperately wanted to check on things at home.

The flapping leather caught the steer's interest and insulted his pride, and he charged. Will coolly inspected the distance to the nearest tree and the space between him and the safety of the corral fence. Both were too far to risk turning his back on the raging animal, so Will stood his ground, expecting to throw himself aside at the last possible instant.

When the separation between Will and the wickedly pointed horns was no more than three body lengths of the onrushing steer, the earth shook once again—an aftershock, a concluding exclamation point to punctuate the power of the original quake. No wavelike rolling motion this time, but a single sharp jerk of the land. Will felt as if a rug were being yanked out from under his feet.

His knees flew upward, and he landed abruptly, sprawled on his back in the path of the steer. Paco and Peter were both jolted out of the tamarack.

Fortunately, the tremor played no favorites: the charging animal was also knocked from his feet. His front legs collapsed under him as if he had run off an unexpected cliff. The force of his rush drove the steer's muzzle solidly into the ground.

When Will got to his feet again, the steer was still struggling to get up from its knees. The ranchero watched the beast warily, but its blind rage was all gone. In place of the infuriated pitching of its horn, the animal shook its great head uncertainly as if trying to clear it.

Still staggering, the steer tottered off toward the creek bottom in search of others of its kind. It moved slowly, testing each footstep carefully before committing to it.

Will called out to ask if his son and the Indian were all right, then whistled a sharp signal. He was answered at once by a familiar neigh. Flotada, the gray horse, trotted obediently back into sight. The gelding's flanks were lathered with a nervous sweat. He rolled his eyes and trembled at Will's touch, as if the quivers in the soil had flowed upward into the body of the horse.

Will replaced the bridle and tightened the cinch, then shouted for his son and Paco to retrieve their mounts and follow as soon as possible. A slight touch of his large-rowelled spurs put Flotada into a gallop.

As he rode, Will saw the signs of the devastation caused by the quake. A stone fence bordering the road was knocked to pieces, and the earthen dam of a stock pond had collapsed and drained out all its water. Will urged the gray to greater speed, until only one hill stood between him and the ranch house. He ran a hand through his red hair and shuddered involuntarily as they passed the crest. He was afraid to see what lay before him.

To his surprise and momentary relief, the two-story wooden home seemed completely untouched. Then the curve of his route brought the rear of the estate into view. He drew in his breath sharply; where the adobe cookhouse had stood, there was only a mound of debris, at this distance not even recognizable as having been a building. Beside the ruins two figures stood unmoving, and lying across the heap of blocks was a splash of color that resolved itself into a familiar form. Will's senses spun and, even though the earth was still, he reeled in the saddle.

Francesca! Will jabbed his spurs into Flotada's flanks, and the gelding cleared twenty feet in a leap straight down the hill, lifting his rider over four rows of grapevines and plunging directly across the flower garden.

Will abandoned the horse's back in mid-gallop and threw himself toward Francesca's body. He gathered her in his arms, and she began to sob.

His wife's disheveled dress, tear-stained face, and bloodied fingers told him all he needed to know. Taking her firmly by the shoulders, Will tenderly set her aside, giving her to Simona and Luis to hold. He lifted a great block, then seized the projecting end of one of the roof timbers and used it to lever up a mass of the rubble.

A shaft of light penetrated into the heap of adobe and landed on a corner of the oak table. One edge was raised slightly; a clear space of no more than ten inches in height was left above the dirt floor. In the small crevice, the top of Don Pedro's bald head could be seen, covered with ashes, dirt, and plaster grit.

Deeper into the pile Will dug until he had uncovered the tabletop. Bending his muscled back and lifting with all the strength of his six-foot-three-inch frame, he raised the broad oak table and tossed it behind him.

He stooped to grasp his father-in-law and pull him free, then stopped with a fierce intake of breath. Francesca cried out again, "Father!" and started forward, but Will gestured sharply for Luis to hold her back.

When the tabletop was removed, the truth was

plain: the lower half of Don Pedro's body was not merely imprisoned by the fallen bricks; it was crushed beneath them.

The old ranchero's eyelids fluttered; he was still alive! Will could not imagine how it was possible. A ragged breath escaped Don Pedro's lips, no stronger than the faint breeze that stirs the cottonwood leaves.

Will held his stiff-brimmed hat so as to block the sun from his father-in-law's face. The change in light brought Don Pedro's eyes fully open. He struggled to focus them for a moment; then a look of recognition came over his face. "Will," he said softly, "Francesca . . . is she all right?"

"Yes," Will reassured him, "she's fine. Save your strength, Don Pedro. We'll soon have you out." Even as he spoke, Will knew it was hopeless.

The old ranchero knew the truth, and he shook his head in denial. "Before my body . . . is . . . released from these clay bricks," he whispered, "my spirit . . . free from its clay." His voice faded and his body stiffened with a spasm of pain, but he fought it down fiercely. "Your fine new home . . . does it still stand?"

Will assured him that it did. "The wooden frame took the shock," he said. "It was not damaged."

Don Pedro gave a nod of satisfaction. "You were right . . . not use adobe," he wheezed, his breathing more forced and shallow now. "Old ways . . . passing. No quedan ni rastros . . . no vestige will remain."

"Papa," Francesca pleaded, "don't leave us!"

Don Pedro rallied once again at the sound of Francesca's weeping. "Kiss them all for me," he said. Then loudly, "I love you, children—" and his words dissolved in a fit of coughing that left a pink froth on his lips.

Gesturing with a twist of his head for Will to lean close to him, Don Pedro instructed, "Move the stones now, and let me pass." When Will complied, a smile washed over the old ranchero's features. His eyes opened wide, and he stared upward into the bright blue California sky.

CHAPTER 2

The dirt was soft and deep along the country lane that wound through the northern stretches of the great central valley of California. The four mules kicked up the earth underfoot in little explosions of red dust, even though the four travelers were moving slowly.

The lead rider was an Indian named Two Strike, a Delaware who scouted for the United States Army. He was dressed in a blue woolen shirt and army-issue trousers, but he was clearly Indian; two shiny black braids rested on his shoulders. Just as clear was the fact that he was a scout; he paid constant attention to the marks in the dust made by previous travelers, and his searching eyes roved continuously.

Following Two Strike were two men dressed in buckskin shirts and trousers and caps made of animal skins. The first was the younger of the two, Anson McBride by name, nicknamed Cap.

The other man wearing the garb of a trapper from the high lonesome was Tor Fowler. Fowler was tall and angular; hawk-nosed and sharp-chinned. As the Indian scout's eyes swept the path ahead, Fowler's senses registered the brush and trees on either side and silently monitored the road behind. It irritated him that the last man in the column kept up a running monologue

21

of comments and criticism about the dust, the slowness of the travel, and the unnecessary caution.

The talker's name was Davis, a settler who had arrived in California by wagon train. He seemed to think that he could tame the West like he handled store clerks back home in the States—just complain loud and long enough, and things would be run more to his liking.

"Hey, Fowler, what's that Injun up to now?" Davis demanded.

Tor Fowler reined in the mule and stopped in the shade of a cedar. Two Strike, the Delaware scout, had abruptly turned off the road and ridden up a hillside above the track to scan the countryside. He stared especially long and hard at their back trail.

"Reckon he's doin' what Captain Fremont pays him for," responded Fowler.

"Huh!" Davis grunted, gesturing with his rifle up toward the hill, where the Indian peered into the distance. "He looks right impressive, don't he? 'Cept, what's he lookin' for? Ain't no Mex within miles of here. Ain't that right, McBride?"

McBride, the youngest member of the Bear Flag brigade, looked worried. "I ain't sh-shore," he stuttered. "We st-stayed on this road a long t-time, an' maybe we oughta get off it."

"Well, excuse me!" blurted a disgusted Davis, slapping his shapeless felt hat against a thigh covered in greasy, patched homespun. "We ain't gonna get back in two days ner two weeks if that Injun stops ever' mile for a look-see . . . an' now this half-wit thinks we should go skulkin' through the bushes all the way to Pope's ranch an' back." His railing stopped suddenly when Tor Fowler fiercely yanked the mule around and rode toward him.

Fowler's eye bored into Davis's round, pudgy face. He hissed in a low, ominous tone, "How'd you 'scape gettin' your hair lifted before this, Davis? Don't never call Cap McBride half-wit again, hear? He's got more sense than you, stutter or no."

Fowler watched as Davis tightened his grip on the Colt revolving rifle. But any reply Davis thought of making never made it past the knife edge of threat on Fowler's sharp features. "All right, all right," Davis muttered. "No call to get riled. You mountain men is so touchy. I just want to get on with it. Thunderation! Them Mexicans will be busted and the war clean over 'fore we get back into it."

"I don't think so," Fowler replied.

"What's that mean?"

The buckskin-clad trapper lifted his chin toward the knoll above the road and the Indian scout still posed there. "That scout . . . he just give the sign for riders comin'."

"T-tor," Cap McBride asked. "Do we r-run or f-fight?"

Looking to the Indian scout again before replying, Fowler said, "Fight, I reckon, unless we can parley. Two Strike says there's riders ahead of us, too."

Fowler had already selected the brow of the hillside that overhung the road as the place to fort up. A lightning-struck cedar had slabbed off, and part of its trunk rested against some rocks near the edge of the cliff. The steep banks and the thick brush back of the spot made the location defensible, at least for a time.

At Fowler's urging, Cap McBride led the mules farther up the hill into an elderberry thicket. Fowler ordered him to remain there to keep the animals quiet while the other three men prepared for battle.

Fowler, Davis, and the Delaware crouched down behind the cedar log rampart. Davis groused about "skulkin' and hidin' from the cowardly Mexicans," and made a great show of his eagerness for a fight. Fowler thought briefly of correcting the settler, reminding him that these were native Californians fighting on their home ground and that the Americans were the invaders, but he decided it was a waste of time.

Also ignoring Davis's rumblings, Two Strike coolly set about inspecting his weapons. The Indian carried a short-barreled gun, sixty-six caliber. Fowler saw the scout carefully lay the rifle in the fork of a tree branch, and set his powder horn and a row of cast-lead balls in a seam of bark beside it. Two Strike also examined a razor-sharp hand axe, checking its edge before thrusting it back into his belt.

Fowler's rifle, bought at the Hawken family gunshop in St. Louis, rested comfortably across his forearm as it had for thousands of miles. He had carried it across the Rockies more times than he could count. This expedition to California was his third trip in the employ of Captain John Charles Fremont. The Hawken had stopped marauding Pawnees, killed grizzlies, and saved Fowler's life more than once.

Fowler watched with amusement as Davis dithered around, looking up the road in one direction and then peering down in the other. The settler alternated between declaring that nobody was coming, spoiling for a fight, and maintaining to the air that the approaching horsemen would be other Americans anyway, since the Mexicans were too scared to face the Bear Flaggers.

"You got that thing loaded?" Fowler asked dryly,

indicating Davis's Colt revolving rifle.

"Huh? Sure enough—fire six times to your one. I bought this new just before I come west with Grigsby's train."

"Ever shot it? You know them newfangled things is dangerous."

Davis looked to Fowler as if swelling pride might overpower good sense, but the echo of cantering hoof-beats shut him up. All three men lowered themselves behind the log as the mounting noise of a large number of horsemen approached.

A dozen riders cantered into view and stopped just below the embankment where the Americans had paused not ten minutes before. Peering through a heap of brush above the level of the cedar log, Fowler examined the enemy troops.

They were a mixed lot, Fowler judged. The two leaders seemed to be a fair sample of the rest of the group. One man was dressed in knee britches of fine cloth and sported a stylish flat-crowned hat. The tack on his well-groomed bay showed silver conchas at every joint and fitting. The man himself was broad of face and pleasant in appearance.

The other man at the front of the column of twos was the complete opposite. His clothing was shabby, and he wore a red bandanna tied over his head and knotted at the back of his neck around his shoulder-length hair. A wisp of scruffy beard clung to his chin. The red horse ridden by this second man was a fine tall animal, but the mochila cloth covering the saddle frame was an old, stained blanket. As the sorrel danced about in the roadway, the mark of Sutter's brand could be seen on its flank. *Stolen, I'll be bound,* Fowler thought.

The rest of the riders were divided between these two extremes—some were well-dressed young caballeros, and others were lean and hungry-looking men with knife-scarred faces. In only one respect did the groups match: none had modern-looking weapons. Some carried old-style muskets and obsolete flintlocks. The rest were armed with lances or pistols only.

The lean man with the scraggly beard spoke, loudly enough that the watchers on the hill could hear. "Don Carrillo," he addressed the well-dressed middle-aged man in Spanish, "the trail of the Americano dogs stops here. They have either turned aside into the woods or doubled back. I told you we should have moved faster. We must find them and exterminate them."

There was a general murmur of assent from the group, but the man addressed as Don Carrillo disagreed. "Juan Padilla," he said, "we wish to capture the Americans, but it is more important to interrogate them, find out their intentions, than to execute them; and General Castro has so ordered. Please remember this."

"Bah!" spat Padilla. "If you have no stomach for this business, then go back to the women. All *true* Californios wish to teach these rattlesnakes a lesson they will never forget."

"You dare to speak thus to me?" countered Carrillo. "You saloonkeeper!"

This is getting interesting, Tor thought. A little dissension among the Californians would make a worthwhile report to Captain Fremont.

"Don't puff up with me, señor rich ranchero. Remember, I was elected co-captain of this troop of lancers."

So intently was Tor Fowler listening to the plans of the troop's next move that he did not see Davis rise up from his kneeling position and slide the Colt over the top of the log. Davis spoke no Spanish, but the settler had correctly concluded that the richly outfitted Carrillo was an important man.

The sound of the single-action hammer being cocked drew Fowler's attention. He threw himself toward Davis, but too late. The roar of the sixty caliber rifle discharging deafened both men as they crashed against the trunk of the tree.

Don Carrillo reeled in his saddle and dropped like a stone to the dusty roadway. "Emboscada!" the horsemen shouted, and the battle was joined. Two Strike's gun fired and a lancer threw up his hands and screamed. A flurry of shots replied from California muskets.

Tor rolled back to his position, picked out a man aiming a pistol and fired. A third horseman clutched his leg, and Padilla shouted, "Retreat, amigos, retreat!"

The fleeing horsemen fired a few shots back over their shoulders, but none took effect. They soon disappeared out of sight around a bend of the road.

Exultant at this victory, Davis jumped up on the cedar log and yelled catcalls after the Californios. "Look at 'em run! What'd I tell you? They won't even stay to fight. Did you see me drop that fat one? Right through the brisket and—hey, why'd you jump me?"

Tor Fowler seethed with rage. It was all he could do not to club the ignorant settler where he stood. "You cussed fool!" he said through gritted teeth. "You may have killed us all. Now get that popgun reloaded and get ready."

"Ready for what? We won, didn't you see? They run off with their tails betwixt their legs."

"They'll be back. By now they figured out that they heard only three different guns, and they know right where we are."

Tor stopped suddenly as he heard a distant rumbling sound and saw a swelling dust cloud floating up above the trees. Both the pounding noise and the swirling haze swept nearer.

When the rank of riders reappeared, they were six across the front, all bearing lances ready. The shafts may have been old and dull from disuse, but the triangular steel points glittered in the sunlight. The churning mass of men and horses surged forward like a single spike-toothed beast bent on the destruction of the Americans.

In contrast to the now-cowering Davis, Tor stood upright and took careful aim. At extreme range he fired and saw a palomino horse stumble but come on. He remained standing still, reloading mechanically as he picked out his next target.

When Two Strike fired, a Californian slumped forward. His lance struck the ground, pitch-poling the man out of his saddle and under the hooves of the onrushing horses.

Davis fired all six chambers, hitting nothing. His fingers fumbled as he tried to reload and he scattered percussion caps across the tree trunk. Two chambers received no power, two got double charges, and two got powder but no shot. Tor ignored him.

The wave of riders swept closer, urging their mounts up the steep bank without hesitation. The second rank spurred past the bend of the road, then wheeled to attack from the other direction.

A lancer's plunging bay reached the top of the embankment. Instead of jumping over the cedar log, the caballero turned sharply and rode along it, lance point at the ready. Tor fired, and then, with no time to reload, used the Hawken as a club and knocked the lance head aside as the Californio charged past.

Out of the corner of his eye, Tor saw Davis futilely squeeze the trigger on two misloaded chambers. After the two empty clicks, Davis threw the Colt and fled up the hill toward the mules.

At the opposite end of the fallen tree, Two Strike faced a musket with his hatchet. As the rider cantered up the brow of the embankment, the Delaware leaped at the horse's head. It reared up, eyes rolling in terror, and struck out wildly.

One of the flailing hooves knocked Two Strike to the ground. As the Indian struggled to his feet, another Californio rider appeared above the barricades, his pistol aimed at the scout's head.

Two Strike gave a defiant yell and spun the hand axe at the attacker. He missed, and the shot pierced his heart and sent him hurtling down the embankment.

Just that suddenly, it was over. Fowler lay on the ground, a lance thrust against his throat.

Flanked by lancers and followed by a third man with a musket aimed at his head, Fowler stumbled down the embankment and was forced to kneel in the churned dust of the road. Beside him lay the bodies of the leader of the Californios, Don Carrillo, and another man.

Raising his head wearily at a new noise from the hillside, Tor saw Cap McBride prodded down the hill.

"Q-quit stickin' me," Cap protested. "I'm a-g-goin'."

Glad to see that Cap at least appeared unharmed, Tor asked, "What happened? Did they get Davis?"

"N-no!" Cap said with disgust as he was likewise forced to his knees. "He weren't even hurt. He r-run up and kicked me out of the way and r-rode off with all the mules!"

"Silencio!" the man known as Juan Padilla shouted. He spurred his prancing sorrel in a tight circle around the kneeling men.

"Four Fingers," Padilla said to the rider who had killed Two Strike, "how many did we lose?"

"Two killed and four wounded, Capitan," was the report.

"All right," said Padilla abruptly, "shoot that one first." He indicated Cap McBride.

"Hold on!" erupted Fowler in Spanish. "He wasn't even in the fight; and anyway, you don't shoot prisoners!"

"Not all at once," sneered Padilla, shaking Davis's Colt rifle in Fowler's face. "You we may tie to horses and pull apart. What do you say to that, miserio?"

Tor Fowler pleaded for the life of his friend, who was being dragged over toward the earth bank at the roadside. "Prepare to fire," Padilla ordered.

"See you in g-glory," Cap called to Tor. Musket fire rang out, and McBride toppled face first into the road.

With an anguished groan, Fowler dropped his head to his chest. Anticipating his own death, he did not see and barely heard the riders approaching at a gallop.

"What is the meaning of this?" boomed a commanding voice at the head of the newly arrived troop.

"Ah, General Castro," whined Padilla. "We were ambushed by Americanos, but we have defeated them."

"Padilla," Castro warned, "do not trifle with me. By whose order are you executing prisoners? Answer me!" he thundered.

"Don Carrillo's," Padilla lied. "He who was murdered by the first treacherous shot."

"Well, no more," Castro demanded. "The remaining prisoner is coming with me."

CHAPTER 3

Northward, the dark green heights of the rounded peaks shimmered in the haze. To the south, a curious trick of the atmosphere caused the low hills of the island of Santa Cruz to loom over the settlement of Santa Barbara as if lying only a short swim away instead of twenty-five miles off shore.

The grass-covered knoll that overlooked Don Pedro Rivera's rancho was itself a tiny island, set between the mountains and the sea. Francesca thought for perhaps the hundredth time that it was in just such a place that she fully understood her father's love of California and his desire to remain and never return to Spain.

As a young girl she had often climbed to this very location to dream of her own future. Through the changing seasons—from wild flower spring to peaceful summer and on into blustery fall and gentle winter—she had grown into a reflection of the beauty and charm of her California home.

The breeze off the ocean was rising, and it ruffled the black lace veil covering Francesca's face as she stood beside her father's newly dug grave. An obelisk of pink granite already marked the spot. Don Pedro had lovingly dedicated this hilltop years earlier when Francesca's mother had passed away.

Her father and mother had come together to the knoll to take the children on outings, to plan the building of their house, and to speculate on their future and that of their chosen homeland. Now they would lie together, side by side, in that place of beauty and peace.

Francesca was flanked by her tall, broad-shouldered husband on one side and her slender son on the other. Their three other children, all younger than Peter, were away at the missionary school in Hawaii. Beside Peter stood his two best friends, the sixteen-year-old twins, Ramon and Carlos Carrillo. Across the grave from her was her brother, Ricardo, his wife Margarita, and their stairstep brace of six children.

At the foot of the grave, a small man in the garb of a Catholic priest led the group of bereaved in the Lord's Prayer. The cleric's diminutive stature and dark brown skin and eyes displayed his Indian heritage.

The small circle of family was surrounded by a much larger group of mourners that included Don Andres Pico, the governor's brother, and Don Abel Stearns. Stearns, a Yankee-born trader, had been living in southern California for almost twenty years and was reputed to be the richest man on the West Coast. He was so widely admired and respected that he had been named subprefect of the pueblo of Los Angeles.

When the service concluded, Don Andres and Stearns drew Will aside. "Don Will," Don Andres said, "we hate to intrude upon your grief, but serious matters have arisen which require that we speak with you."

"Don't fence with him," said Stearns gruffly. "Straight out, Reed, do you know anything about this ragtag bunch of Americans calling themselves the Bear Flag Republic?"

"Only the same rumors that everyone has heard—some American adventurers have proclaimed independence from Mexico. I also understand that some U.S. army officer has been encouraging them, but again, it's only hearsay."

"Exactly!" Don Andres burst out, his elaborate side-whiskers bobbing. "It's all hearsay and rumor, promoted by General Castro in Monterey. Listen to this official proclamation." He extracted a folded paper from a deep side pocket of his frock coat and read: *"Countrymen, arise, Divine Providence will guide us to glory."*

"You see," Stearns explained, "we in the south believe that this fuss may be a pretext for General Castro to increase the size of the militia, ask Mexico City for more troops, and subdue all of California with himself as dictator." Stearns wiped perspiration from his broad forehead with a silk handkerchief, and loosened the knot of the black cravat tied below the stiff-winged shirt collar.

"This is all very interesting," said Will, looking to where Francesca stood hugging Margarita, "but why tell me? You are, as you say, intruding on a time of sorrow and I have never been interested in politics."

"Quite right," apologized Don Andres, bowing.

"Hold on," Stearns said in a no-nonsense tone. "Let's get it all said at once; then he can give us a straight answer. Will you go see the American captain and find out the truth? Fremont's his name, and he's been across the Rockies with surveyors and mountain men like yourself. You two should speak the same language."

"No," said Will with finality. "It does not concern me or mine."

———

The guard almost shot Davis before recognizing the shambling, gasping form that lurched out of the darkness. The round-faced settler's clothing was torn and full of burrs and foxtails. He was weaponless and walked with a limp, clutching under his arm a crutch improvised from a tree branch. His face was streaked with blood and his hair matted with dried gore from a gash that cut across his forehead and angled up into his scalp.

The guard alerted the camp of the Bear Flaggers. He caught the swaying Davis and led him to the watch fire. Whistling a low exclamation over the settler's injuries, the sentry pressed a cup of coffee into Davis's hands, then brought a bucket of fresh water to wash the wound.

By this time a crowd had gathered around the scene. "What happened, Davis? Where are the others?" asked Andrew Jackson Sinnickson. At five foot ten, and solid as a brick wall, Sinnickson was the leader of this group of the Bear Flag Party.

"Dead," said Davis, shuddering with the horror of the memory. "The Mexicans jumped us. I fought my way clear, but they killed all the others. It was terrible. There must of been fifty of 'em. 'Kill all Americanos,' they was yellin'!"

Sinnickson looked around at the blackness of the Sierran foothill night. "Double the sentries," he ordered, "and put two more men on guard around the horses."

"Got shot in the head," Davis said, indicating the scalp wound. "Shot me clean outta the saddle. I crawled into some bushes and hid out all last night and hiked back here today." There was instant acceptance of this story, although the truth was less dramatic. When Davis had ridden away from the fight, he had looked over his shoulder for pursuers once too often and turned back just as the racing mule had run under a low tree limb.

"Tor Fowler and Cap McBride and the Injun all dead?" said Sinnickson, shaking his head in sorrow and disbelief. "Well, it can't be bloodless now. Grigsby, you and Merritt best ride on over to Captain Fremont and tell him what's happened. Tell him the country's up, and we are requesting the army's aid. Davis," he continued gently, "can you remember any more that might be helpful—anything at all?"

Davis tried his best to look noble and heroic, but only partly succeeded, since he winced at the touch of a washrag on his forehead. "We stood 'em off to start with—yessir, turned 'em back. Ouch! Watch it, will you? An' I heard Fowler say that I had killed a feller name of Car-ill-o or Ka-reyo or somethin'."

"Jose Carrillo? Why, he's a rancher in these parts and supposed to be a moderate man. Was he with them?"

"Right enough," David concluded. "He was their leader."

———

Captain John C. Fremont ran his slender fingers nervously through his wavy brown hair, then plucked at the top brass button of his dark blue uniform. "So you say hostilities have begun?" he asked Sinnickson, the black-haired leader of the Bear Flaggers.

"Yessir, and it wasn't us who started it, neither. Oh, we had rounded up some horses and made some plans, defensive like, but now it's a real shooting war. We've even had reports that General Castro is advancing against us with a force of six hundred. We need your men and your leadership, Captain."

Fremont looked at Marine Lieutenant Falls. "This puts me in an awkward position, doesn't it, Lieutenant? You see," he explained to Sinnickson, "war is imminent between the United States and Mexico over the annexation of Texas, but it has not yet begun. If I, as an officer of the United States Army, allowed my troops to be used against the Mexicans, I would be committing a breach of international diplomacy."

Sinnickson looked uncomfortably nervous. His prominent Adam's apple bobbed several times before he spoke. "But you can't leave us without protection. We're American citizens, after all. Why, the blood-thirsty Mexicans shot and killed three men in cold blood without any provocation. They may attack our women and children next! You've got to help us!"

Clearing his throat politely, Lieutenant Falls waited for Fremont to acknowledge him. "What is it, Lieutenant? You have a solution?"

"Yessir, I think so," the short, round-shouldered officer said in his whiny voice. "If Mister Sinnickson would step out of the room for just a moment?"

After Sinnickson had obliged, Falls continued. "Sir, the exact wording of the verbal instructions for you from Secretary of State Buchanan was that you were to render aid to American citizens in the event of actual hostilities. Do you hear the wording, sir? Not in the event war is declared, but hostilities. Isn't that what has just happened, sir?"

Fremont brightened visibly. "You're exactly right," he agreed. "My duty is plain. Lieutenant, ask Mister Sinnickson to come back in, and the others as well."

When the group of Americans calling themselves the founders of the Bear Flag Republic had assembled, Fremont explained his conditions for assisting them. Fremont was to be the absolute commander, with all others subject to his orders.

"The first order of business is to capture General Castro. We must strike quickly and not give them time to gather their forces. Those Californio leaders who have already surrendered will remain in custody at Sutter's Fort. From here on we need to move too rapidly to be encumbered by prisoners."

———

Trading ships of many nations—French, Russian, English and American—had all plied the California waters for decades. Some were legally approved by the Customs House in Monterey. Many more were smugglers' crafts, anxious to take advantage of eager buyers and hundreds of miles of unpatrolled coastline.

As commerce increased, countries encouraged the fair treatment of their citizens by shows of naval might. The British and the Americans in particular kept Pacific squadrons cruising the length of California. It was even rumored that Britain might accept Upper California in payment of old war debts owed by the Mexican government. Of course, officially, Britain had no interest in any stretch of the Pacific coast south of the Oregon territory, and her ships were supposedly present as observers only.

The appearance of Her Britannic Majesty's Ship-of-the-Line, *Juno,* caused no little stir when it anchored off Santa Barbara. Although not as impressive as the eighty-four-gun British frigate, *Collingwood,* which was also sailing in California seas, the *Juno's* three decks, bristling with cannons, were an imposing sight.

"What do you make of it all, Father?" Will Reed asked the small-statured priest who had spoken at Don Pedro's funeral. "First, Governor Pico arrives from Los Angeles with eighty armed men, and now this war-ship." The two watched from the white sand beach in front of the sleepy coastal town as *Juno* sailed into the lee of the point before turning sharply upwind and let-ting go the anchor with a show of British precision.

"My friend," said the dark brown little man, "as to the governor, there is no reason why I should know any better than you; and yet, as regard to the English ship, I believe I have the answer."

The ranchero waited for the explanation as the priest debated about saying more. "You always think more than you speak, Father," Will urged him good-naturedly.

Resuming his reply with a grin and a shrug, the priest offered, "I have been informed by my superiors that a certain priest, a Father McNamara, is to be ex-pected here. As his last location was reported to be Ma-zatlan, where the British fleet has been anchored, I have followed the rabbit tracks to the rabbit hole and come up with a rabbit."

"Father Francis," laughed Will, "there are times when you still sound more like Blackbird of the Woilu

Yokuts than you do a Catholic priest!"

"I am proof," said Father Francis modestly, "that one may be both."

"And you said your visitor's name is Mik-Na-Mee-Ra . . . is he Yokut also?"

"No." Father Francis shook his head, smiling. "Another tribe . . . Irish."

Three gently waving lines of white breakers separated the landing of Santa Barbara from its anchorage. Will and the priest watched as the small boat, called the captain's gig, was fitted out and two men, one in the robes of a cleric and the other in a naval uniform, were rowed ashore.

"And will you be entertaining the visitor?" Will asked.

"No," said Father Francis. "Since attacks by the shaking sickness and by the Mojave tribes have moved my people up into desolate hills, they have many needs. I go now to serve them."

CHAPTER 4

The gold braid on General Castro's uniform was frayed and faded, and one of his tunic buttons was missing. Even his mutton chop whiskers and gray hair looked thin and threadbare.

His voice was not worn out, though, as he shouted in English at Tor Fowler with a bellow like an angry bull. "Where is Fremont going? What are his plans?"

Fowler was seated in a stiff wooden armchair, his hands bound behind his back with rawhide strings. The chair's legs were uneven, so Fowler rocked forward and back with each blast of the interrogation.

"Don't know, General," he answered truthfully. "I signed on to hunt meat for the camp and to keep track of Injun sign. Never was any call for anybody to tell me nothing important."

Castro seemed impressed with the frankness of Fowler's reply and changed topics. "How many men are armed? What about more troops?" he shouted.

With a look of complete sincerity, Fowler lied, "Man, General, you just can't believe it! Must be close on a thousand in camp already and I heard the lieutenant sayin' that General Kearny was comin' with a thousand more."

Castro rocked back on his heels as if he were the one

seated in the wobbly chair. A look of worried conster-
nation ran across his face, and his bushy eyebrows
pulled together. The effect was so comical that it took
all Fowler's poker playing ability to keep from laughing
out loud.

Switching to Spanish, the general addressed the
scrawny killer, Juan Padilla, who stood at his elbow.
"What do you think, Padilla?" the general demanded.
"Is he speaking the truth?"

"We have seen nothing like a thousand men, General," Padilla replied. "But let me tickle his ribs with
this," he drew a knife halfway out of the dirty sash knotted around his waist, "and I'll have the truth soon
enough."

Castro made an abrupt gesture to Padilla to put
away the blade. "He may prove useful as a hostage later.
In any case, you do not know this breed," he said. "His
kind live with the Indians and think like them—they
will die without speaking and spit blood in your face
at the end."

———

The first rifle shot came just as General Castro's
camp was stirring for breakfast. Tor Fowler had spent
an unpleasant night, unable to swat the cloud of mos-
quitoes that feasted on him. He was standing, tied with
his back to an oak tree, his wrists fastened by a rawhide
strap that encircled the trunk. At the whine of the bullet
and the report of the gun, he sat down abruptly and
slithered around to put the oak between him and the
firing.

The Californios bolted out of their tents and made
a rush for their stacked weapons. The first man to reach

the muskets was dropped with a rifle ball through his leg, and the rest suddenly elected to flop on their stomachs and crawl. Three men ran toward the corral of horses, but two were picked off trying to climb the rail fence, and the third crouched behind a post.

General Castro stormed out of his quarters shouting commands. As Fowler watched, Castro attempted to buckle his sword belt around his middle before hitching up his suspenders and got tangled up. A bullet clanged into the hanging lantern in front of the general's tent, and he dropped, sword and all, behind the oak chest that contained his belongings.

In quick succession, two bullet holes were added to the trunk's fittings. One split a leather strap and flipped the loose end up in the air. Another neatly punched out the lock.

The Californios were returning fire with their muskets, but it was plain that the Americans were out of range of the older weapons. Buckskin and homespun-clad figures could be seen walking upright between the trees at two hundred yards distant. A blue-garbed man with a white bandanna tied over his head was waving men into positions.

"Whooee!" Fowler yelled. "Go to it, boys! Hammer and tongs!"

Another bullet clipped a branch above Fowler's head and knocked some leaves and bark down around him. "Hey, General," he called, "how about untying me?"

Castro scowled at him and shouted for his men to circle behind the corral and saddle up.

Working the rawhide binding, Fowler sawed the tie back and forth in an attempt to set himself free. The Californios were feverishly occupied, so escape never looked more likely than now.

Sixteen lancers made a crawling circuit of the corral and managed to saddle their mounts among the jostling and milling horses. Fowler figured that they would make easy targets riding through the gate, since it was too narrow to allow more than one at a time. But he had not counted on the Californios' resourcefulness—or their horsemanship.

With a shout of defiance, four jinetes, expert riders, jumped their horses over the corral fence without bothering about the gate. These were followed by four more and twice again four until all sixteen riders swept across the camp and the open pasture toward the Americans. The tiny pennants on the lance heads waved like flags when the horses jumped, and then fluttered in front of the riders when the weapons were leveled for the charge. Fowler looked on with fascination as the lancers galloped into the hail of rifle bullets now being fired with renewed intensity.

Back and forth Fowler continued sawing at the leather tie until his wrists were bloody. "May have to cut this tree down before I get loose," he muttered to himself.

Another fusillade of shots made the scout look up again and sneak another view around the tree trunk. Two riders were shot out of the saddle, and when one horse was hit, he made an end-over-end roll at full speed. The power of the charge was broken short of the American positions, and the riders were forced to seek shelter in the trees bordering the pasture to try to regroup.

The action by the lancers had succeeded in drawing the Bear Flaggers' attention away from Castro's camp, giving the general time to organize a second wave of horsemen to go in with muskets while he and the rest of the Californio troops withdrew south toward San Francisco Bay.

Still sawing feverishly at the leather strap, Fowler heard another flurry of shots, and two more thudded into the tree behind which he hid. He yanked with all his strength on the rawhide and suddenly jerked up as another bullet unexpectedly hit the binding, freeing him instantly.

The mountain man wasted no time trying to untie his ankles. With his feet still bound together, he began crawling quickly toward a clump of yellow mustard brush just beyond the edge of the camp.

Fowler just reached it when he heard the unmistakable sound of a hammer click. A cold barrel poked him in the ear. It was Padilla with the Colt rifle captured from Davis. "I would like very much to kill you," the wiry little man said with a twisted grin, "but General Castro says you are to come once again with him."

The solid wooden wheels of the ox cart bumped violently over the tiny rocks and dropped with a thud into every pothole. Tor Fowler wished that his captors had tied him into the carreta standing up. As it was, each bounce sent a jolt up his tailbone like being thrown from a mustang onto a granite boulder. Fowler was being transported with the cavalry troops' supplies: sacks of beans, spare saddles, General Castro's trunk, and one prisoner, all clumping along together.

Fowler listened with amusement to the groaning complaints of the ungreased axle. Without their Indian servants, these Californios seemed incapable of the least effort that required manual labor. He had heard it said that if a task could not be done on horseback, then they would not do it at all. At any rate, not one of these horsemen had attempted to grease the axle, even though a bucket of tallow for that purpose hung underneath the carreta.

The cart bumped down a track that ended at a broad expanse of dark water. Fowler guessed it was San Francisco Bay, although he had never seen it before.

General Castro rode up the column on his white horse. "Padilla," he yelled, "take the prisoner and your men and go across the bay. I want Fremont to think that I have gone that way also, but my men and I will ride south from here, driving before us such horses as we can find and recruiting some more lancers."

"Couldn't we sweep around the road and attack Fremont's flank?" Padilla asked. "Do we have to run, General?"

Castro looked thoughtful. "It is the best strategy at present," he said, "until we have raised the whole country and that cursed snail Pico sends us more men. We are not ready to face Fremont's thousand."

Tor Fowler had to duck his head quickly to hide his smile.

———

Lieutenant Falls stood on the shore of San Francisco Bay not far below the town of San Rafael. He was noisily sucking his buck teeth as he shook his head with displeasure. "It's a bad job," he remarked to Davis. "Castro and his men have escaped across the bay. Now they'll have a chance to regroup—perhaps fortify San

Francisco. What I wouldn't give to know his plans."

The breeze blowing across the water was tossing choppy little waves up on shore. Gusts danced on the wide expanse in playful patterns. The wind rippled a stretch of surface half a mile wide, leaving smooth and undisturbed swaths on either side. The passing clouds floating overhead contributed to the show of shifting light and shadow, dividing the waters of the bay into green and blue areas that changed with each moment.

Shading his eyes with a dirty palm, Davis peered across the bay. "What's that?" he asked at last.

"Where?"

"Yonder, straight across from us. See that white patch? First I thought it was a wave and then I figured it for a cloud, but now I reckon . . ."

Falls confirmed his guess. "It's a sail, and it's headed right this way, too. Let's get out of sight and see where she lands."

The two men hid themselves behind some rocks above the makeshift pier that served as a landing for San Rafael. It was not long before it was apparent that the triangular sail on the little sloop was tacking so that it would arrive right in front of them.

———

As the single-masted ship spanked against the tops of the waves, drawing closer to the shore, Falls could see that two men paced the forepart of the deck and a third handled the tiller.

"Slide out toward the road," Falls ordered Davis. "Bring back as many of our boys as you can round up quickly, but do it quietly. Stay out of sight till I holler, in case they've got a bunch below deck. But when I yell, come on up and take 'em."

The fore-and-aft sail fluttered in the breeze and the small ship lost headway, but not much. The last two tacking movements swung the boat away from the pier and then back parallel to the shore. Falls thought that the pilot was going to run alongside the end of the dock, leaving his escape route ready for a quick departure. The sloop's motion toward the pier looked to Falls like a fleeing bird swooping toward a tree branch. The two men on the forward deck had taken places along the rail on the landward side.

The sail dropped and the sloop coasted up beside the wharf. The first man jumped over the rail and landed cleanly. He pivoted suddenly to catch a carpet-bag that the other tossed to him. Then it was the second man's turn to leap. His foot snagged some rigging and he tumbled onto the planks of the dock, but he was up quickly as the boat continued to glide past the pier.

The ship's departure was as abrupt as its arrival. Falls watched as the lone remaining figure hoisted the sail taut again and put the tiller over. The two men left standing on the dock each raised a hand in farewell, but the steersman did not acknowledge them. The sloop stood out into the bay sharply, as if dropping off the passengers had been an interruption to the important business of sailing.

Falls drew his pistol and cocked the hammer, glancing down to check the percussion cap. The two Californios moving up the pier were young and carried no weapons openly, but Falls was not taking any chances of running foul of something hidden in the carpetbag.

A moment passed, and in the brief interval the sloop

was out of range to be hailed into returning, but the men had not yet reached the landward end of the pier. Stepping out from his place of concealment, Falls leveled his pistol at the chest of one and commanded, "Halto! Or whatever means stop in your lingo."

Startled by the lieutenant's sudden appearance, the pair who had been talking and laughing paused mid-stride and were silent. They made no attempt to flee. Both lifted their arms in token of surrender, one holding the carpetbag awkwardly at shoulder height before he set it down. Lieutenant Falls looked from one face to the other and thought he was seeing double. They were twins, about sixteen or eighteen years of age. Dressed alike in black knee breeches and short black jackets with silver trim, the brothers matched down to the silver buckles that decorated their boots.

"Señor," said one, tentatively lowering his hands and stepping forward.

"Get back there!" snarled Falls, "and keep your hands up!" The round bald patch on the lieutenant's head turned bright red when he was angry, or scared; it was crimson now.

"Señor," the young Californio meekly tried again, "we speak English. Please to tell us what is wanted— what have we done?"

"I'll ask the questions around here, and you'll answer right sharp if you know what's good for you. What are your names?"

The one who had already spoken continued to reply. "I am Ramon Carrillo and this is my brother Carlos."

"What are you doin', slippin' in secret like this?"

The twins glanced at each other, and then Ramon said, "The manner of our arrival was not of our choos-

ing, señor. The captain, he was afraid to come at all—
we had to pay double—and even then we had to jump
because he would not stop."

"Yeah? What's he afraid of?"

"He said some crazy Amer . . . some foreigners had
caused some trouble on this side of the bay and he did
not wish to get mixed up in it."

"Davis!" Falls bellowed, "bring 'em on down. We
caught us some spies!"

"Oh no, señor," protested Carlos. "We are coming to
visit our uncle, who lives near Commandante Mariano
Vallejo in Sonoma."

"Vallejo, eh?" sneered Falls, scratching his thin gray
mustache. Davis and half a dozen men with rifles ran
up and surrounded the Carrillo brothers. "Well, Vallejo
is already our prisoner, and his rancho and his horses
belong to us. What do you say to that?"

The twins said nothing at all. Falls, certain that
their silence proved their guilt, and puffed up with
pride at the capture, ordered the carpetbag dumped
and the brothers searched.

"Lookee here, Lieutenant!" Davis exclaimed as he
drew a folded sheet of paper from Ramon's jacket
pocket. "Some kinda handbill or somethin'."

"Lemme see that," demanded Falls, snatching the
paper away from Davis. Falls scanned the printing;
then, since he could not read Spanish, he announced
the only thing he could make out for certain. "It's
signed by General Castro hisself!"

"Well, go on, Lieutenant," requested one of the other
soldiers of the Bear Flag brigade, "read it to us."

"It says . . ." Falls paused; then he plunged ahead.
"It says for all Californios to take up arms to kill Amer-

icans! Yep, that's what it says. Men, women and children, it says, kill 'em all. Burn their homes, take their belongings, run 'em clear out of California. That's what it says!"

Ramon and Carlos both reacted with horror. "Oh no, señor!" they exclaimed in unison. Then Ramon continued. "It calls on Californios to forget their past differences and band together to fight the invaders, but it says nothing about—"

"There, you see?" said Falls triumphantly. "They admit it! Out of their own mouths, you heard 'em. They were sneakin' across the bay to organize a counterattack—probably to slaughter us all in our sleep!"

"String 'em up!" growled Davis.

"Drown 'em like mongrel pups," suggested another.

"Run!" yelled Ramon, pushing Falls to the ground. He lowered his shoulder and ran into the midsection of a second of his captors before a rifle butt clubbed him to the ground.

Carlos threw himself off the pier and into the chilly waters of the bay. Striking out strongly, he was swimming along the shoreline when the first rifle ball struck him in the back. When the second and the third crashed into his head, he sank without a splash.

"Davis," Falls asked as they stood over Ramon's unconscious form. "Name Carrillo mean anything to you?"

"You bet," said the settler, rubbing the half-healed wound on his forehead. "Carrillo was the name of the leader of the bunch that jumped Tor Fowler and me. . . . I killed him," he concluded proudly.

"Well, what do you know? This scum here is some kin to that feller," nodded Falls, nudging Ramon with the toe of his boot.

"What do you want we should do with him?"

Falls considered a moment. "Captain said we got no time for prisoners," he said. "Drag him over in that gully and shoot him. And remember, they was spies and assassins!"

Tor Fowler had a theory about pain. He believed that one could withstand anything by concentrating all thought somewhere else. It seemed to him that pain could not rob a man of his reasoning without his agreement. If he would just ignore it, then he could go on functioning and surviving.

He had tested his belief before, once when a barbed Pawnee arrow had to be cut out of his back. Another time he had hobbled ten miles across a range of eight-thousand-foot peaks on a newly broken leg. *Keep on thinking and live, or give in to the pain and die.* In Fowler's mind, it was that simple a choice.

But he had to admit that the present torture put a whole new slant on pain. He was hanging face downward, spread-eagle by rawhide straps around his wrists and ankles. The straps were tied over the rafter beams of an adobe hut so that his body sagged under its own weight and tore at his shoulder joints. His breathing was labored and slow.

Concentrate! Ignore the pain! Fowler forced himself to review how he had gotten to this place; but he had almost lost track of how many times his captors had moved him, by forced march on foot and in the carreta, and most recently in the smelly hold of a little trading sloop.

They had thrown him headfirst into the bilge of the

small ship and carried him across the bay to the tiny, dirty settlement of Yerba Buena. Upon arrival, Padilla had ordered that Fowler be trussed up like a ham hanging in a smokehouse.

Now that Tor thought about it, there was one thing to be grateful for. The Apaches practiced a similar torture to what he was undergoing now, but with an additional refinement: they hung their victim's head downward over a slow fire.

CHAPTER 5

Will and Francesca were invited to a reception honoring Father McNamara and the *Juno*'s captain, Blake. The evening's festivities were held at the property of the little Irish doctor, Nicholas Den.

Den stood at the front of the receiving line, enjoying his role as host and introducing the rancheros and merchants to Father McNamara and the warship's captain.

At the opposite end of the row of dignitaries was Governor Pio Pico. With his politician's smile firmly in place on his coarse features, and his ample girth stuffed dangerously into a formal black suit, Pico managed to look jovial and imposing at the same time.

Nicholas Den fairly bounced with the importance of the occasion and, as often happened when the small curly-haired Irishman got excited, his Spanish took on an improbably Irish brogue.

"Don Will and Doña Francesca Reed," he intoned with a ferocious rolling of *r*'s.

McNamara spoke a cultured Spanish as befitted a well-educated man. "Charmed, Doña Reed," he said, bowing. "Don Reed . . . American, yes?"

"Mexican citizen these last sixteen years," replied Will. "And you . . . Irish, like the good doctor here?"

"Aye, but a long way from home, and a long time

away as well." McNamara was a large man, as stout as Governor Pico, but a head taller. He had pale skin, much freckled from the California sun. His short brown hair was balding in the crown, and Will thought he looked like a woodcut of Friar Tuck in a book about Robin Hood.

"Father McNamara is here to speak with the governor about Irish colonists coming to live in California," interjected Den with excited self-importance.

Father McNamara shrugged off the comment. "Ireland, my homeland, has many starving folk and not enough farmland to feed them, while I hear that California has plenty of good soil for willing hands to cultivate. But I am really here on a mission for the church."

Will and Francesca passed down the row and reached the governor. The Reeds had met Governor Pico many times before; and while Will did not entirely trust the politician, he had at least a grudging respect for the man who governed as a Californio first and not as a high-handed representative of the government in Mexico City.

"Eighty soldiers escorted you here, Governor?" Will inquired. Pico, beaming through his thick lips at a row of señoritas coyly peeking at him from behind their fans, pretended at first not to hear. But he could not ignore the topic when Will continued. "Two years ago we took up arms against a governor who brought his army with him from Sonora, and we kicked him and his men back south again."

Pico's stubby fingers plucked at the gold and black onyx watch chain draped across his expansive stomach. He was not pleased with the questions, but he attempted to cover up his displeasure by answering lightly, "You will remember that I also participated in the ouster of Governor Micheltorena. Now another man's ego may have gotten too big for him, but I assure you, it isn't mine."

"So you believe that the stories of the American invasion are exaggerated by General Castro for his own purposes?"

"It remains to be seen how much of the present crisis is General Castro's invention. But rest assured, Don Will—whether to put down rebellion or to corral General Castro, I and my men are ready to march." His words were uttered in a light, almost careless tone; and he made a sweeping gesture with both arms, like a bear hug, as he said the word *corral*.

"And the timely arrival of the good captain and the British warship?" added Will, indicating Blake, who was listening without comment. "Does that event also have something to do with the crisis?"

"Purest coincidence only," Pico laughed, holding his ample sides as if to keep the humor confined. "The *Juno*, on which Father McNamara was coming to visit me, put in at San Pedro, only to hear that I was on my way here. Captain Blake was kind enough to sail on to Santa Barbara instead of making Father McNamara await my return to Los Angeles. Ah," he interrupted himself, "I see dinner is ready."

———

"Hogwash," muttered Will to himself in English.

"¿Cómo?" asked Francesca, looking cool and beautiful in her white dress. "What did you say?" Her eyes were twinkling, and Will knew she had not only heard his comment but understood it as well.

"Nada—nothing, really. I am just wondering what is so important about a scheme to bring in Irish settlers that Pico would lie about it."

"How do you know he is lying?"

"Because," Will said, pausing in the doorway and leaning close to Francesca's ear as he pretended to straighten the red sash knotted around his waist. "Because Blackbird—Father Francis—told me that Father McNamara was expected here. That means Governor Pico and the Irish priest planned to meet here in Santa Barbara all along."

Enormous quantities of food greeted the guests as they entered the dining hall. Quarters of beef, roasted over oak-coal fires, were sliced into huge steaks and heaped on round wooden serving trays the size of wagon wheels. The Indian servants who carried the trays around the dining hall staggered under the weight of them.

Fragrant mounds of arroz con frijoles—rice and beans, seasoned with chili peppers—were accompanied by steaming heaps of freshly baked corn tortillas. The diners sampled the Zinfandel wines from two different mission vineyards; some from vines already over fifty years old.

At length the still-heaping platters and serving bowls had been carried around a final time and the last filled-to-capacity guest had refused even one more helping. The pewter dishes were cleared away, and the tables and chairs were pushed back to make room for the musicians to come in and tune up.

Will and Francesca went for a walk in the plaza, as did several other couples. "You won't get sleepy before the dance, will you, Señor Reed?" teased Francesca.

"Not a chance, Señora Reed," Will asserted earnestly. "What with you being the most beautiful woman present, I'll have to be on my guard that some young caballero doesn't sweep you away."

"Impossible!" she said, stretching up to kiss him quickly. "I am holding on to the most dashing and handsome man here, and I won't let him go. I saw the eyes that shameless Julieta was making at you."

"Huh!" Will scoffed. "Making eyes at old Pico, I shouldn't wonder, or that British captain."

"I do so wish Peter could have come this evening," Francesca reflected. "He will be sorry he missed the dancing."

"He is being sensible," Will argued. "Since he is leaving tomorrow to join the twins in Sonoma, he needed to stay home this evening to prepare. You know, he is writing out a list of instructions for the care of his herd of cattle during his absence. I like to see him taking his responsibilities seriously."

"So like his father," Francesca murmured.

"And his grandfather," Will added. "Don Pedro would be proud."

The first notes of the jota sounded from the band, calling the strolling couples back to the dance. Will noticed the glint of a tear in Francesca's eye. He guessed that the swirling mixture of violin and guitar conjured up for Francesca visions of the Aragon of her ancestors. No doubt the mysterious strains that drew from the Moors and the gypsies called to her mind the Spain she had never seen, only heard about in the stories of her father's youth. Now she would hear them no more.

The inner circle of ladies faced the outer circle of men. Handclapping and energetic footwork punctuated the jota, the dance that translated as "little details." Pio Pico capered around the dance floor, sweating profusely.

At the next break in the music, Will made his way to the punch bowl. The laughing governor was there ahead of him, with a young señorita hanging on each arm and every word. "Quite a nice fandango, eh, Governor?" said Will in an cheery, offhand way.

"Most excellent," Pico agreed. "Nicholas certainly knows how to entertain. For being a little chino, a curly-headed Irishman, he has become more Californio than many who were born here. Not like some foreigners who think to bring their own culture and force it upon us."

"Perhaps the new crop of Irish will fit in as well," Will observed.

"No doubt, no doubt," agreed the governor, looking anxious to return to the dance floor where the strains of a waltz could be heard.

"Isn't it curious that Father McNamara says his plan is of little importance, and yet it could not wait for your return to Los Angeles?"

Pico was starting to get annoyed. "I don't know what you are trying to suggest, Don Will Reed, but this is a strange line of questions for a man who told my brother and Don Abel Stearns that he had no interest in politics."

"Let us say that I have no political *ambition*," said Will, stressing the last word while staring into Pico's flushed face. "But that does not mean I lack concern for my country."

"Which country?" shot back Pico. "Mexico or the United States?"

"California," Will retorted, bristling.

A cry from the musicians' corner rang out over the laughing crowd. "The bamba! The bamba!" Applause and still greater laughter greeted this announcement.

Three wicker hoops the size of small wine casks were placed in a cleared area of the dance floor. Three young señoritas stepped forward, and each stood inside a hoop. Each was handed a glass of water to balance on her head.

A single guitar began to slowly strum a rhythmic progression of measured notes and minor chords. The girls dipped gracefully and carefully brought the hoops up to knee level. The tempo of the music picked up as each dancer moved first one ankle and then the other in a succession rapid enough to keep the hoop from slipping down. The glasses jostled, but not a single drop of water was spilled.

Faster and faster went the chords as the crowd picked up the beat by clapping their hands. Each girl bent quickly and gave the hoop a spin; the flashing ankles and pointed slippers were joined by the whirling of the bands. One girl, trying to keep up the pace of footwork and manage the spinning hoop, overbalanced and the water glass tumbled off her head. A groan came up from the audience, but it changed to a cheer as the dancer recovered quickly enough to catch the glass before it struck the floor.

The two remaining girls were well matched, and the spectators placed wagers on which would last the longest. The noise of the crowd and the music and the clapping drowned out the staccato sound of horses' hooves ringing on the paving stones of the plaza. None of the partygoers saw the two lathered horses clatter up to the mission in the darkness, nor observed the two men fling themselves to the ground as their mounts slid and skidded to a stop.

Through the rear of the milling throng pushed Peter, calling, "Father!" The crowd, grumbling, parted reluctantly, jostled by the interruption.

Paco shoved two onlookers roughly aside and received angry glares in return. Someone muttered curses about Indios who did not know their place. Another uttered a threat of punishment.

The music was reaching a climactic moment when Peter pushed into the inner circle of the audience and spotted his father and mother on the other side.

"Father!" Peter yelled. "Ramon and Carlos are dead—killed by the Americanos!"

The music jerked to a halt. The crowd noise died away gradually, and then as the message sank in, one of the dancers screamed. In the abrupt silence that followed, the shattering of the water glasses on the stone floor seemed to ring on and on.

———————

The slash of the leather strap across Tor Fowler's back made him jump and yank against the rawhide that tied him to the roof beams. He gave a grunt of pain when the blow landed, but otherwise he made no sound. The sweat of his torture gathered in the tightly knotted furrows of his brow and dripped from the end of his pointed nose onto the black earth of the floor.

Padilla had beaten Fowler before, but this whipping was particularly savage. The former saloonkeeper, Padilla, was matched blow for blow by his accomplice Four Fingers. In between lashes the two men reviled Tor, telling him he deserved death for what the Yankee pigs had done.

The mountain man was grateful that the cutthroats did not beat him in silence. Even though he did not understand what they were talking about, it helped him to ignore the pain as he tried to cipher out their accusations.

He gathered that some of the Bear Flaggers must have killed two young Californios ... in cold blood, from the sound of things. This news gave Padilla an excuse to be even more cruel than usual.

Finally the pace of blows began to slacken, as Fowler knew it would. The Californios tired of their activity and stopped the beating. Fowler knew what was coming next and braced himself for it.

The knots securing the rawhide ties were let go and he was dropped, face first, onto the floor. Padilla kicked him twice in the ribs and told him to crawl back to his corner, but Fowler could not move. The Californios grasped him roughly and pitched him back to the wall like a discarded cowhide.

Sometime later, an old crone of an Indian woman came into the adobe hut. She brought Fowler a pan of brackish water and a shallow bowl of thin barley gruel. The woman, who never spoke, much less answered questions, fed the broth to Tor like a baby and held the tin of water to his thirsty lips. It would be several hours before he could use his arms again.

"It does not require the gift of prophecy," Father

McNamara declared to Governor Pico, "to foresee that California will not remain part of Mexico forever . . . unless some defensive measures are undertaken."

"Yes, yes," nodded Pico impatiently. "Everyone agrees that the American invasion is real and not merely an invention of General Castro's. But what do we do now?"

McNamara looked pointedly at the stoic face of the British Captain Blake and finally received a nod of agreement. "Give us one square league, 4000 acres, for each family and we'll plant a hedge of Irish Catholics strong enough to keep the Methodist wolves at bay."

Pico's bulging eyes turned inward toward his bulbous nose as the strain of mental calculation took place. "You want me to deed . . . 4 *million* acres of land? That's preposterous! In all the area around all the existing pueblos and missions, there is not that much unclaimed property!"

McNamara shook his head and in an ingratiating tone replied, "It is not necessary to disrupt your fine coastal cities. My people are people of the land, willing to settle in the harsh interior. What is it called . . . the valley of the San Joaquin?"

"But it is completely uncivilized . . . a country of wild Indios and wild beasts!"

"Exactly," agreed McNamara. "Ideal for both our purposes, don't you agree?"

Pico pondered. "For such a large transaction, I must confer with the territorial assembly—"

"By all means," the priest concurred. "Only remember, the wolf is at the door, howling to be let in among the sheep. May I suggest at least your tentative approval while the details are being worked out?"

Pico nodded eagerly and stuffed his too-small European style top hat down onto his large head. He bustled from the room, shouting for his carriage driver to bring the caretela. Father McNamara turned to regard Captain Blake. Broad smiles painted both of their faces. "He doesn't yet understand how completely he has just thrown his lot in with us, does he?" Blake said. McNamara shook his head, still smiling. "But the assembly?" Blake questioned. "Will he be able to get them to agree?"

"Without question. Exchange worthless, unoccupied land for a buffer of one thousand settlers between the ravenous Americans and these pitiful remnants of bygone Spanish glory? My dear captain, we could have asked for 40,000 acres for each family, and they would still agree."

Captain Blake nodded his understanding. "Of course, it doesn't really matter that it would take a year or more to arrange such a colony. The first twenty British subjects will want protection from the American invaders, and the British navy will be honor bound to oblige."

"And what better way to aid and protect than to seize the ports?" McNamara said. "Will it be difficult to locate twenty volunteers for such a project . . . facing wild Indians, wild beasts, wild Americans, and wild Californians, I mean?"

"You have only to ask," Blake replied. "I have *already* dispatched twenty sailors whose ill health made them eager to exchange their shipboard labors for a little time spent living off the land."

"Captain," Father McNamara asked with delight, "where did the governor put that bottle of excellent

California brandy? I think a toast is in order."

"Don Abel Stearns wishes to speak with you, Father," reported Peter from the head of the stairs. Will, who was digging through an old sea chest in the attic of his home, turned at the interruption.

"Did he say what he wanted? I am in a terrible hurry, Peter."

"I know, Father, and I told him so, but he insists that it is important."

At that moment, Will's hands grasped the leather-wrapped parcel he had been seeking. He stood up with the rolled bundle. "All right," he said, "now I have what I was looking for. Tell him I'll be right down."

Don Abel was admiring the striking clock on the mantel of the Reeds' fireplace. Will gestured for him to be seated in a chair made entirely of cattle horns lashed together with rawhide.

"Don Will, I know you are anxious to go north and locate the killers of Ramon and Carlos Carrillo, so I will be brief."

Will acknowledged the accuracy of Don Abel's statement with a nod, but said nothing and waited for the merchant to proceed.

"I want to . . . how can I put this? I want to encourage you to go to Captain Fremont with an open mind."

"An open mind about murdering children?" Will burst out. "What are you saying?"

"No, no!" cautioned Don Abel hurriedly. "I mean, I am certain that Fremont is an honorable man and that he will also want to punish the offenders. I hope you will give him a chance to investigate."

"And I hope it will already be done and the murderers under arrest!" snapped Will. "If Fremont has any control at all over that rabble, he should have captured the killers already."

"Correct, correct," said Stearns, "but please remember that the future of this land is properly with the United States and not with Mexico. We don't want Captain Fremont to think that our sentiments run any other way."

"Is that what this visit is about?" Will snorted, standing up abruptly. The leather-covered bundle fell off his lap and spilled its contents: a fringed buckskin jacket and leggings from Will's days as a mountain man. "You think I might make Fremont rethink his support for the revolt? You know what, Stearns? You're absolutely right! If I find out that he or any of his men had anything to do with the murder of the Carrillos, I am going to tell him that all Californios, Yankee or Spanish, will resist him and the so-called Bear Flag rebellion to the last drop of our blood!"

"You cannot be serious," Stearns responded. "We want to belong to America—peacefully, if possible, but by armed conflict if necessary. How can you, an American yourself, feel any differently?"

"Stearns." Will towered over the hawk-nosed man. "You have had your beak in the account books for too long. You cannot see anything but stacks of silver reals. Get out of my house."

Stearns went without protest. Will stood glaring at his back as he left, and his son, who stood in the entryway, closed the door behind Don Abel with somewhat more force than was necessary.

"Peter, I am leaving you in charge of the herds," Will said.

"But I want to go with you," his son replied. "They were my friends."

"I know," Will agreed, "and it is hard for you to remain behind, but it is important. Paco is a crafty mayordomo, and he will help you do what is required."

CHAPTER 6

Six days after the terrible news about the twins had reached Santa Barbara, Will Reed stood on a hill overlooking the little settlement called Yerba Buena. Located on the tip of the peninsula that formed the western enclosure of San Francisco Bay, it was not much more than a miserable collection of shacks and huts. Initially it had sprung up around a Hudson's Bay Company trading post, but had never grown into a thriving city.

The small harbor that provided the anchorage for Yerba Buena was a cove on the eastern shore of the peninsula, just below the ramshackle town. The only ocean-going ship anchored there was a Russian vessel down from Alaska. Its rigging looked dull and in disrepair, and an air of greasy neglect hung over it.

Will arrived seeking answers, but found no one to provide them. All the Mexican authorities had fled southward, including General Castro and his men. The alcalde of Yerba Buena had abandoned his post and taken to his heels. He had heard that the Americanos not only killed children but that they took captured officials and skinned them alive.

No one seemed to know anything about what had actually happened to the Carrillo twins. Leidesdorff, the American vice-consul, was conveniently absent. Robert Ridley, the captain of the port and a Britisher who had adopted California as home, was likewise ignorant of what was happening north of the bay. The Americans were victorious, it seemed, and all of northern California now belonged to them.

Will made up his mind to cross the bay and seek out the American commander. He would demand an explanation of the deaths of the brothers and insist on knowing what was being done to catch the murderers.

But no one would take him across the water. Trading sloops and fishing smacks were available for hire, but no Californio captain was willing to risk coming in range of the American rifles. Will had even offered to pay the captain of the Russian vessel for passage, but the oily-looking officer had only stopped stuffing his face with rice and beans long enough to say that the matter would have to be referred to Sitka and that a response would take six weeks.

In frustration at his wasted day, Will climbed the windy heights above Yerba Buena just as the sun began to set. He stared hard across the straights. Shielding his eyes against the glare on the water, Will traced the line from the cove below him to the far shore, lit in gold and orange by the reflection of the sinking sun.

There was a sail on the horizon. As Will watched, the small craft, no bigger than a whaleboat or the shore launch off a trading vessel, tacked on its course toward the peninsula. The ranchero decided that here at last was someone who had braved the trip to the farther shore at least once and could perhaps be persuaded to go again. Will started down from the heights, leading Flotada by the silver-worked bridle. He paused again on a slightly lower ridge, expecting to see the boat veer around toward the harbor.

Instead of coming to land at Yerba Buena, the vessel grounded directly below the old presidio of San Francisco. Twelve men armed with rifles jumped from the boat. They held their weapons aloft to keep them dry as they waded through knee-deep water, picking their way over rocks to the shore. The last to step from the boat was a young man, clean-shaven, with a thin face and wavy brown hair that showed around the edge of the blue cap he wore. He was dressed in a blue shirt and a fringed buckskin vest.

The men formed into two columns and hiked up the hill toward the presidio. The young man, who was apparently the commander, walked between the two files, carrying a rolled up banner. As Will watched with disbelief, the leader stepped to the center of the compound of tumbledown, crumbling adobe walls and unfurled an American flag. As the twelve men stood respectfully still, the commander evidently spoke some official words that Will could not hear. *Taking possession*, Will thought, and he shook his head at the audacity.

Will's approach to the gate of the old fort was stopped by a man in the uniform of a United States Army lieutenant. There were two guards with the officer, one wearing a long, loose coat of deerskin, knotted around the waist with a rawhide tie. The other had on a shirt of homespun above the dark knee breeches of a sailor, and no shoes.

"Hold it right there," ordered the lieutenant. "Who are you, and what do you want?"

Looking past the odd assortment of men, Will could see small groups of men clustered around the antique brass cannons with which the presidio was armed. The sounds of clanging hammers filled the evening air as the squads of invaders set to work spiking the ancient guns.

"Maybe you didn't hear me? Or is it that you only habla español?" said the lieutenant roughly.

"I speak English or Spanish as needed," Will replied, "but I only speak *with* the commander—take me to him."

The army officer stepped up a pace and peered at Will from his flat-crowned hat to his tooled cowhide boots and silver spurs. "What do you know," the bucktoothed little man observed to no one in particular, "he dresses Mex and talks American. What are you, anyway?"

"Why don't you stop wasting my time?" said Will angrily. "My name is Will Reed. I am related to the two young men, Ramon and Carlos, who were reported killed by the Americans. I am here to find out who was responsible."

Lieutenant Falls looked over his shoulder. Captain Fremont, the man in the fringed vest, was returning to the small boat waiting at the shore. The captain was already out of earshot. "Will Reed, eh?" Falls repeated with a sideways glance from his beady eyes. To the two men with him he remarked, "Stubbs, Bender . . . I think he's a spy . . . take him, boys!"

The soldiers stepped toward Will, expecting to close in from both sides, but he surprised them by jumping straight for the lieutenant. Bearing Falls to the ground, Will jammed a knee hard into the officer's belly. Falls doubled up with an explosion of breath and feebly waved for help.

Stubbs, the man in the sailor pants, grabbed Will from behind, pinning Will's arms to his sides. Will let himself be yanked upright, then he stomped down with all his force on the attacker's bare foot, raking his spur down the man's shin at the same time. With a howl of pain, Stubbs let go his hold and clutched his wounded leg while he hopped around on the other.

Grabbing up his Lancaster rifle, Bender swung it around toward Will. Too close to bring the gun to bear, Bender tried to club the ranchero with it.

Will seized the barrel of the rifle with one hand and clamped his other fist firmly over the hammer to prevent the gun from being fired. A tug-of-war began in earnest, but Will's extra height and superior strength was winning the battle for possession almost at once. Unable to let go for fear that Will would shoot him with his own gun, Bender did the only thing he could think of: he screamed for help.

It took a moment for the terrified shouting to penetrate the ears of the squads still pounding away at the two-hundred-year-old cannons. Peering through the gathering gloom, the raiding party was astonished at the spectacle at the gate. The lieutenant was still on the ground, fumbling with the flap of his holster and gripping his stomach. Stubbs was also sitting on the ground, holding his lacerated knee and moaning. Meanwhile, a big man in Californio dress wrestled for Bender's rifle. "Help!" yelled Bender again. "We caught us a spy!"

Will saw the others drop their hammers and reach for their weapons. He drew Bender up on tiptoe with a sudden jerk upward on the rifle. Planting his boot in the middle of Bender's chest, Will kicked the shorter man backward twenty feet.

Will made no attempt to shoot the rifle. Spinning sharply around, he sprinted for the gate where his ground-tied horse patiently waited.

Just as Will swung into the saddle, Falls freed his pistol from its holster and fired. The fifty-four caliber ball hit Will just below his right elbow. The impact almost flung him completely over the offside of his horse. He reeled in the saddle, snagging the rowell of his spur in the cinch as if riding a bronco. The gray bounded off toward the village of Yerba Buena.

––––––––

The door of Fowler's adobe hut prison creaked open. Someone stood in the doorway, but Tor Fowler did not raise his head from where he hung face downward in the rawhide straps. The pattern of his imprisonment was set, and he no longer feared torture or expected rescue.

The mountain man knew that Padilla was carrying on with the torture only because he had the power and enjoyed inflicting the pain. There was no real expectation that Fowler would furnish any important information. Fowler also knew that Padilla would stop short of killing him. As long as General Castro wanted Fowler kept as a hostage or for a future prisoner exchange, his life was safe.

A blow on the side of his head swung Fowler against the adobe bricks and his skull bounced off the wall. Muscles that he had thought already numbed to pain awakened at the renewed violence.

A second clout on the head set Fowler's body rocking

in the rawhide thongs like a tenderfoot riding a green-broke colt. His moccasined feet thumped against the back wall of the hut and his angular frame began a corkscrew motion.

The third blow whizzed past his ear but did not strike him. Fowler's mind could not grasp why this was so until he heard Padilla's voice, so slurred and thick with drink that the words were almost incomprehensible.

The missed swing had spun Padilla completely around; he tripped over his own feet and sprawled on the floor. Tor's sharp features dangled only a few feet overhead and Padilla mumbled, "Gonna slit your throat, gringo." The Californio pulled his long knife from the sash around his waist and waved it clumsily in front of Tor's nose.

Fowler forced himself to speak calmly and reasonably. "General Castro will not like this—not one bit. You know he told you to keep me safe."

Padilla's unfocused eyes followed the arc of the glittering blade as he waved it in a gesture of denial. "No, no, gringo," he said in a surprisingly soft voice. "*No importante*. The general would not want me to let you escape. If you are killed escaping, what can he say?"

When sober, Padilla was capable of any evil. He was totally without conscience; he stopped at nothing, except for fear of punishment. Now it seemed that the drink had taken that last restraint away.

The rawhide cords suspending Fowler left him hanging at just the right height to have his throat cut. As soon as Padilla could stagger to his feet, it would all be over, unless . . .

Fowler recalled the blows of a moment before. His

feet had brushed against the adobe wall. He was that close, and the leather straps had more slack in them. For his plan to work, Padilla needed to be standing close by. Fowler thought he knew just the appeal that would work.

"Do not kill me," Fowler pleaded. "If you took me back to Captain Fremont, he would pay you gold. Two hundred dollars."

Padilla shook his head. He jabbed the point of the blade into the earth and tried to lean on it, but fell back. "Bah! No scout is worth that to his commandante. I am tired of wet-nursing you, gringo. Make your peace."

"Wait!" Fowler said in an urgent tone. "Listen to this—I know where there is gold hidden—more gold than you ever dreamed of—taken off a rich ranchero that we killed."

Padilla's spinning eyes steadied and he blinked slowly and deliberately as if trying to wake up. "Another Yankee lie to save yourself," he sneered.

"No, I swear it. Only one other man besides me knew of it, and he's dead. If I die it'll be lost forever. Don't you know the Valdez rancho? The old man's gold is buried, and I know where. Let me down and I'll give you half."

Drunken reasoning told Padilla that a man who was lying to save himself would promise all of a treasure, not merely offer half. And Don Valdez was known to be a wealthy ranchero. It was just possible. . . . He stood clumsily and took a step toward Fowler's head. "Do you know what will happen if you are lying, gringo?"

"Yes," said Fowler urgently. He kicked his feet upward hard and bent his body in the middle, ignoring the sudden tearing in his muscles.

Fowler's feet contacted the rear wall and he pushed off with every ounce of force left in his abused carcass. As the forward motion began, he ducked his head.

Directly on target, Fowler's thick skull connected with Padilla's face, which had been only inches from his own. The single blow propelled the Californio backward through the air, until the flight was cut short by the other adobe wall.

Padilla hit heavily, and Fowler heard a crack as the Californio's head struck the bricks.

Between the impact of Fowler's head used as a battering ram on Padilla's chin, and the short arc of the Californio's body that ended against solid adobe, the man was unconscious before his frame pitched forward into the dirt.

Now, how to get free before someone else came, or before Padilla was awake again? Otherwise, Fowler had only postponed the inevitable.

———

The outcry of pursuit rang in Will's ears, and several more shots were fired after him into the gathering twilight. One splintered against the bricks of an old well just as he rode past, but no other came close.

The shooting fell silent; the Bear Flaggers were too busy running after their quarry to reload. But their speed on foot was no match for Flotada. The great gray horse bounded over a gully and turned up a barranca. The narrow canyon between the two hills dropped mount and rider below the sight of the pursuers as if they had disappeared into the earth.

Will trusted the horse's instincts to keep him away

from the chase. His own senses were dulled with the shock of the wound.

The houses of the eighty inhabitants of Yerba Buena were scattered and haphazardly placed. Few streets existed at all, straight or not. The gray horse sensed the need to hide their trail, and he darted from crude hut to adobe home, turning corners without Will's commands. Flotada changed directions three times, always when some structure was between his master and the panting pursuers.

Yerba Buena was deserted. At the sounds of gunfire coming from the direction of the already rumored invasion, those who lived in the little community by the bay elected to stay indoors. Flotada turned two more corners, then entered a narrow passage between a larger building and a small adobe shed.

The last abrupt change of direction proved to be too much for Will's precarious hold. His spur's rowell snapped free of the cinch and he tumbled out of the saddle. Making a last grab for the apple of the horn was futile: he swung his injured arm in a desperate attempt to hang on, but his nerveless fingers brushed uselessly against the leather. He fell heavily onto packed earth.

The gray horse stopped immediately, pawing the ground in an anxious declaration of their need to get farther away. Will tried to rise, pushing himself up on his good arm, then falling back when it collapsed under him. Flotada stamped again and whinnied softly.

Squinting against the pain, Will caught sight of a wooden door hanging from leather-strap hinges. The opening led into the hut that seemed to be a shed or storeroom. "Have to do," Will muttered softly to himself.

He dragged himself upright with the last of his strength, knowing he would not be able to mount the horse again. It was all he could do to yank his Hawken rifle free of the leather scabbard and slip the pouch containing powder and shot from around the horn. The world swayed in a dizzy, looping spiral. "Go! Go!" he roughly urged the horse, "get on with you!"

He flicked the cord of the shot pouch at Flotada, smacking it sharply across the horse's rear. The unexpected rebuke turned Flotada's own nervousness into flight, and Will could hear the gray cantering off down the hill.

Will did not wait to watch the animal's departure. He tucked the rifle awkwardly under his good arm and held its stock pressed tightly against his side as he faced the sagging wooden door.

Will kicked it inward, and thrust the barrel of the rifle forward into the room. When no protest erupted, he stepped inside and leaned wearily against the planks of the door as he shut it behind him.

It took his eyes a while to adjust to the darkness of the shed; then he swung the rifle around and fumbled with the hammer to be certain it was cocked.

The unconscious figure of a man was crumpled against the wall of the hut, almost under Will's feet. He looked and smelled drunk. But it was not this man that riveted Will's attention. He focused instead on a buckskin-covered form that hung suspended in the center of the room like a recently slaughtered deer hung up to be bled.

Will could feel the creeping numbness of the shock and pain of his wound sweeping over him. Even reminding himself about the grim chamber in which he had taken shelter did not enable him to shake off the deepening weariness. He was just about to surrender to unconsciousness when a groan escaped from the hanging figure . . . the carcass that Will had thought was a corpse!

The noise pulled him awake with a start. "Who are you and who did this to you?" Will asked in horror.

Fowler's head jerked upward, his eyes snapping open in the gloom at the question Will had asked in English. "For the love of God," Fowler sputtered, "get me down, Mister!" Will searched the folds of his sash for his knife, but it had been lost during his wild ride. "There . . . on the floor by his hand," Fowler urged, "Hurry!"

Will found Padilla's blade, and with the backhanded slash of his uninjured left hand, he severed the rawhide that held Fowler's feet. The mountain man cried out as the sudden extra weight hit his shoulders and his legs refused to hold him up. "Sorry," Will muttered.

"Just get me loose," gritted Fowler.

Another awkward backhand sweep of the knife, and Fowler dropped to the earth with a thud and a groan. He lay so still for a time that Will wondered if the man had died. Will's own body had now expended its last reserve, and he sank to the floor himself, cradling his wounded right arm.

At last Fowler rolled over onto his back. "I hope you got somethin' to cover that snake there in case he wakes up," he urged. "Else I'll have to crawl on over and slit his throat like he was fixin' to slit mine." When Will did not acknowledge this gruesome warning, Fowler called to him again, "Hey, friend, you all right?"

Through pain-leadened lips, Will said, "Arm's broke
. . . shot . . . I'm all played out."

Fowler whistled his dismay.

CHAPTER 7

The sun was finally sinking after a dusty, day-long cattle drive. Peter Reed stood upright in his stirrups and scanned the hills ahead of the trail. He paid particular attention to the gap up ahead toward which he and the Reed vaqueros were moving the herd. The upper reaches of Canyon Perdido touched the wilderness heights of San Marcos Pass.

Grizzlies were not as plentiful as they had been in years past, or so Will Reed had told his son. Of course, according to Will's campfire tales of the early days, every canyon had held an oso pardo gigantesco, a great ferocious bear. In legend, each weighed over a thousand pounds and the track of every clawed foot measured eighteen inches in length! Peter chuckled as he recalled the shuddery excitement of his father's stories.

Still, Peter kept a watchful eye on the places where the live oaks, called *encinos*, grew the thickest. Beyond San Marcos Pass, which loomed ahead, the land was wild and rough and little known to the Californios, whose ranchos hugged the coastline. The other side of the mountains was a place of coyotes, rattlesnakes, and condors, and a home from which the grizzly stirred to raid the cattle ranches. Somewhere up ahead lay the seldom-used trail that Peter's father had followed in first coming to Santa Barbara.

Peter could see no immediate danger threatening the herd of two-year-old steers, so he reined aside and waited for Paco to catch up. Already taller at fourteen than the short-statured Indian, the difference in their heights was exaggerated by the mounts they rode. Peter's grulla, crane-colored, gelding towered over Paco's mule.

"I saw you looking over the ground before we brought up the herd," commented the Indian. "It is well to be watchful in this country. It is a place of bad medicine."

The boy looked curiously at the mayordomo. "You speak like one of the Wild Ones instead of like a good Christian, Paco. Are you superstitious?"

"No, only cautious," Paco replied, crossing himself. "I think that evil is real and does linger in some places . . . places it would be best to avoid if it is possible, but which should on no account be entered blindly."

"Why here?" Peter questioned, gesturing toward the slopes covered with coyote brush and chaparral. "This canyon looks no different from many others hereabouts."

"My mind remembers this place," Paco said, reining up and pointing toward a tree-topped mound near the rocky wall of the canyon's mouth. "It was just there that Don Ricardo, your uncle, was almost killed by an oso pardo before your father saved him."

Nodding his acquaintance with this piece of family history, Peter said, "I have seen the scars on Tío Ricardo's forehead, sí. But the story did have a happy ending. Besides, it brought my mother and father together. Surely you do not believe that the spirit of the bear lingers on here."

"No, no," Paco shook his head, "but it is not just the bear. You see, I was also present on that day. I heard your uncle scream ... saw your father face the oso grande alone, and ... I fled."

The boy hardly knew what to say or how to respond to this. "I never heard that," he said at last.

The Indian said solemnly, "Don Will is a good man, a great man. He told no one, and have I not been his mayordomo these ten years past?"

In a bend of the canyon, the trickling stream had collected in a pool deep enough to water the herd. "We'll camp here tonight and push over the pass tomorrow," Peter announced; then he looked at Paco with embarrassment. "That is, if you agree, mayordomo."

"No," Paco chided, all the uneasiness of the earlier conversation left behind, "you do not appeal to me for approval. Your father put you in charge of this drive. You have made your decision, Don Peter. If I have comment, I will offer it, but as it happens, you have chosen well."

The other vaqueros brought up the herd and set the leaders to circling. The forward motion soon ceased, and the rangy cattle fell to browsing the grass on the banks of the creek.

Paco pointed out a particularly handsome reddish-brown colt in the caponera, the string of horses. "What do you think of the retinto-colored one? The one there with the curly coat?"

Peter knew that the question was not a casual one. His education in horsemanship had begun as a two-year-old, when his chubby legs had stuck straight out from the horse's back and Paco had walked alongside to hold him upright. Questions about an animal's conformation or habits or training were a kind of test, and a game that Peter enjoyed playing.

The retinto with the curly coat had a long, sleek body and long legs to match. The arch of his neck and the set of his shoulders indicated good bloodlines for a horse that would rein well. The colt's large eyes were interested in his surroundings, and he pricked up his ears when a steer splashed into the creek to graze on the other side.

Peter considered all the factors and gave his judgment. "When he comes into his own, he will be one to ride all day without stopping, and he seems attentive."

"Good," Paco confirmed. "You saw that he has amor al ganado—cow sense. It cannot easily be taught, but a horse that comes by it naturally will leap on the trail of one steer and never lose it."

"And now, mayordomo, why did you call my attention to him in particular?"

"Because, hijito, little son, he is broken to the jáquima, the leather noseband, but has not yet worked in the bit. Your father and I wish you to school him."

Mentioning Peter's father made the request into a command. It meant that Will and the head vaquero had planned this lesson before the drive had even begun. Peter knew that the schooling would not be the horse's alone.

———

By the time the camp was set, the herd settled, and the simple supper of beef jerky and hard biscuits finished, the glow of the Milky Way filled the California skies.

The night herds were posted, and Peter was just

drifting off into sleep when the first sliver of the full moon crept above the ridgeline. As if at a signal, a mountain lion screamed in the barranca, upstream where the canyon narrowed into a rocky gorge.

Peter's eyes snapped open and he slapped his hand down on his blanket, over the saddle carbine that rested beside him. "Gently," cautioned Paco from his bedroll nearby. "You will frighten the cattle more than señor Puma."

Apart from a lone bawling steer, the herd remained quiet. There was none of the confused snorting and bellowing that foreshadowed a stampede. "How far away was that?" Peter asked.

A drowsy reply confirmed that Paco felt no danger. "Far enough. The horses will give the warning if he gets near enough to scent. You may depend on it. Of course . . ." Paco's voice trailed away.

"Of course what?" Peter demanded.

The sleepy afterthought was slow in coming. "Of course, if the lion calls near our camp again tomorrow night, we will have to hunt him."

"Why?"

"Because," came the slurred answer, "on the third night, he will be hunting us."

On that cheerful thought, Paco drifted off to sleep. Peter was counting another set of a thousand stars when it was time for him and the mayordomo to go on watch.

———

It was the strangest kind of three-way race, and only one of the contestants even knew about the contest. Tor Fowler studied the unconscious Padilla and the silent figure of Will Reed. Fowler's arms and legs were shot through with fiery pains as circulation returned to his numbed limbs.

Inch by agonizing inch, Fowler stretched out his arms. He dragged his uncooperative body toward Will Reed's weapons. Two feet more to go, one foot, a half. Fowler's fingers closed around the stock of the Hawken rifle. But the weight of Will's body held the rifle prisoner, and Fowler could not jerk it free.

The knife must be his objective then. The room was pitch dark, and Fowler scrabbled in the filth of the hut's floor. He found Padilla's knife near the end of Will's outstretched hand.

Using the weapon to assist him, Fowler plunged its blade into the earth and pulled himself up to it. The dark mass that was Padilla stirred and groaned, and Fowler redoubled his efforts. Like a sailor climbing the tallest mast in the midst of a raging gale, Fowler drew himself hand over hand toward his enemy.

When Fowler was an arm's length away, Padilla's eyes flickered, then opened. For a moment they focused on nothing at all; then Padilla screamed in terror. Fowler knew what Padilla saw: the dark shape of a wild beast with blazing eyes and raking claws that had crawled out of his worst nightmares and was coming to rip out his throat!

The Californio's hands fumbled for a weapon, but found none. Padilla gave a bleat of panic and threw himself backward against the adobe wall just as Fowler stabbed the knife downward.

Fowler struggled to stand. A guttural animal noise came from his throat as he slashed the air again and again. Padilla hurriedly groped his way along the wall to the door. Twice he pushed futilely against it without recollecting that it opened inward.

Fowler's blade sliced both the Californio's legs with a sweeping slash. The wound, not deep, was the goad Padilla needed to escape. Throwing his weight against the ramshackle door, he burst it from its strap hinges and fell out into the night.

The mountain man lit an oil lamp and held it aloft to study the man whose arrival had probably saved his life.

"Come on, man," Tor Fowler urged Will. "We've got to get us both some doctorin'."

Will shook his head. "Not together we can't. You can go back to the army for help, but they want to capture me . . . maybe kill me."

"That's some kinda mistake, you bein' American and all. Why would we be mad at you?"

Will reached up with his good arm and let Fowler help him stand. A swirl of dizziness swept over him, but it passed quickly. "Do you know about the Carrillo twins?" he asked.

"Do I? I should say so!" Fowler agreed emphatically. "I was beat plumb near to death while bein' told what child-killin' murderers us Yankees is! But personally, I never met 'em. Reckon it happened after I got took."

Will nodded. He pulled the sash from around his waist and with Fowler's help used it to fashion a sling to support his wounded arm. "Those boys were my god-children," he continued. "I came here from Santa Barbara to get to the bottom of what happened."

"Well, what *did* happen? How'd you run foul of our folks?"

Will explained the circumstances at the presidio and how the lieutenant had been at first hostile and then belligerent.

"That Falls," Fowler grunted. "He's as useless as a saddle made for a grizzly, and just about as likely to get somebody kilt. Fancies himself a real military hee-ro headed for politics . . . hopes to hitch onto Fremont's star."

"Then you understand why I can't go back with you."

"No sucha thing," Fowler insisted. "Falls, see, he ain't Cap'n Fremont. The captain is an ambitious man, but he knows what he's about. " 'Sides, him and me been in some rough scrapes before and I saved his bacon. He'll be bound to hear your say if I tell him to."

Will still looked doubtful, but he agreed that his arm needed attention. What was more, it was to see Fremont that he had ridden all the way from Santa Barbara, and here was a man who could make the connection.

"All right," he said at last. "On one condition. Don't tell anybody except Captain Fremont who I am. Ask him to come and see me at the cantina down the street."

The two men had no more than stepped into the dirt lane when they found themselves surrounded by a squad of marines. Lieutenant Falls presented a carbine at point-blank range at Will's stomach, remarking with obvious satisfaction, "Fowler. Good work. Escaped *and* captured the spy!"

"Not so, neither," protested Fowler. "This fella saved *my* life, and—"

"Poor man is deranged," Falls observed to the marines. "Take the prisoner away."

Will knew that protest was futile and that any further attempt to fight his way clear would get him shot down on the spot. He let himself be led away quietly.

"Lieutenant," said Fowler, thinking quickly, "I'm warnin' you. This is an important fella with a secret message for Captain Fremont. Ain't nothin' better happen to him!"

Falls regarded Fowler and Will with a look compounded of suspicion and cautious self-interest. "Captain Fremont has already departed, leaving me in charge," he said. "All right, lock him up." Then he added in a grudging tone, "*Just* lock him up."

CHAPTER 8

Peter yawned into his morning cup of coffee and stared at the tin platter of cornmeal mush without taking a bite. "Eat! Eat!" Paco scolded. "One cannot conduct the jornada, the cattle drive, without nourishment."

The curly-haired retinto horse was caught and brought to Peter for saddling. "It is a perfect time to try him with the bit," Paco said. "He was first bitted up exactly one month ago, and now it is time to advance his schooling. Every true vaquero knows that the best reining caballos are given the bit in the full of the moon."

Paco watched as Peter examined the mouth of the reddish-brown gelding before turning to the canvas on which were displayed the various bits. The boy chose a silver-mounted bridle. Attached to it was a mild-curved mouthpiece called "the mustache of the Moor" from its drooping shape. In the center of the cross bar were two barrel-shaped rollers made of copper.

"Bueno," nodded Paco with approval. "Exactly the bit with which the retinto has been standing each day in the corral."

The curly-coated horse took the metal bar in his mouth without objection, and soon little whirring noises could be heard. The colt was spinning the copper barrels with his tongue, indicating his contentment.

Peter saddled the horse with care, tightening the center-fire cinch and leading the animal around in the small circle known as the pasos de la muerte, the steps of death. Many a rider had come to grief when a cinch-binding horse came over backward as the rider's weight was added to the saddle.

Removing the silk mascada scarf from around his neck, Peter tucked it into the bridle over the horse's eyes as a makeshift blinder. He did not know if this precaution was necessary, but it was a point of honor to discover the colt's personality and secrets without asking too many questions.

Stepping lightly into the stirrups, Peter mounted and settled quickly into the high-backed, apple-horned saddle. The retinto stood perfectly still in the clean morning air and flicked his ears back toward his rider. Peter adjusted his grip on the reins and nodded for Paco to remove the scarf.

The spur chain jingled once as Peter tapped his heel against the colt and urged it into a walk. The horse wheeled left and right in response to Peter's directions, and he found no trace of obstinacy or rebellion as the horse worked in the bit.

"Shall we start the herd moving?" Paco inquired.

"Por favor. I'll take the colt across the canyon and back to work on his rein. We won't want to try him with the cattle until tomorrow."

"Bueno," Paco agreed, "and perhaps you may be

able to bring back meat for the camp." He handed Peter a rifle, and watched with affection and approval as the boy rode out of sight.

————

The colt took eagerly to the trail, trotting across the creek and looking around him with an intelligent interest. Peter followed the twisting path away from camp and started the horse up the climb that led out of the canyon and onto a mesa beyond.

A pair of finches chattered in the buckthorn brush. The boy instantly recognized their noisy calls and was reminded of the childhood tales told him by his mother. The finch's red breast, Francesca had said, was caused by blood dripping from the brow of the crucified Christ. A pair of the small birds, so the story went, had flown to the head of Jesus on the cross and plucked out the crown of thorns one by one. God allowed the blood to permanently stain their chest feathers as a remembrance of the time when men had no pity on the Lord of Glory, but two of the least members of creation showed compassion for their Maker.

Both Peter and the rust-colored horse turned their faces toward the twittering sounds in the scrub. The colt nodded his head toward their perch, seeming to acknowledge the finches' greeting. "Ah," said Peter aloud, "so you know the story also? We will be compadres, you and I. Also, I like your curly coat. I think your name should be Chino—Curly. What do you think?"

The trail reached the mesa rim and leveled out as it angled across the plateau. The brushy undergrowth thickened, with gooseberry patches replacing the coyote brush. As Peter scanned the dense growth, his attention was drawn to a clump of heavy thorned cover at the base of a huge boulder that jutted out of the landscape like a stone sailing ship set on end.

Peter's eyes traveled past the location, then flickered back again and he studied the berry thicket intently. Was it a rabbit in the brush, or perhaps only the flitting of another small bird that had caught his notice? Both horse and rider stopped and stared, peering at the unseen animal. Slowly the camouflaged outline of a deer bedded down behind the gooseberry thicket took shape. Peter stepped off Chino's back and carefully lifted the Hall saddle carbine out of its scabbard.

Dropping the reins to the ground, Peter stood away from the colt and took aim. He cocked the hammer while judging which set of branches were actually antlers, and where the point of the buck's shoulder was located. The boy took a deep breath and let it out slowly, then took another and held it, just as his father had taught him.

The boom of the sixty caliber rifle shattered the morning stillness. At the sudden explosion, the buck leaped up from the bushes as if by the release of a spring, but Peter had no chance to judge his success. Behind him, Chino reared and plunged, reared again and came down on the reins. The colt jerked away from the abrupt tearing in his mouth, breaking the bridle and scattering silver conchas across the hillside.

The horse snorted with fear as Peter lunged at him

in a grab for the reins. Chino reared again and struck out with a forefoot, and Peter threw himself backward out of the way. The retinto colt whirled then and ran off, back the way they had come.

Peter sat up and watched the horse's flight. He kicked himself mentally as he retrieved the fallen rifle. The hammer had broken off and the stock had two deep scratches in it. From the dirt near a broken piece of rein he picked up a silver ornament and tossed it morosely up and caught it. What would Paco say? Worse, what would his father say? Peter knew better than to fire a gun next to an untried colt. He should have tied the horse to a stump and then moved away before firing, but the horse's good nature and cooperative spirit had made Peter careless. Carelessness got people killed, his father had taught him. Well, Peter might wish he were dead, but he was not, so he had better pick up what he could and hike on back to the herd and face the consequences. Peter hoped that the colt would find his way back, or else the boy would be in even bigger trouble.

With the broken rifle over his shoulder and two dusty silver conchas in his pocket, Peter turned to follow the vanished horse when a thought struck him. He had fired at the buck, but he did not know whether his bullet had struck the animal or not. The boy fervently hoped that his shot had been successful so that he at least would not have to go back empty-handed.

Peter returned to the location from which he had fired the shot. At first he could see no trace of the buck. He placed his feet in the same tracks again and sighted along the rifle barrel toward the gooseberry patch. Nothing was stirring there now. He swung the barrel slowly to the left, tracing the buck's leap and trying to remember where his last glimpse of the deer had been.

He hoped he had either killed the animal cleanly or missed it completely. Now that he was afoot, he doubted if he could trail the buck if it were only wounded; and anyway, he had no weapon with which to shoot again.

Walking toward the brush pile, Peter circled it on the uphill side, in the direction of the buck's leap. He looked in each clump of thorns and weeds as he passed, but saw no sign that the deer had ever been there, much less had been shot. Peter glanced back at the point from which he had fired, judging the correctness of his course and the amount of distance he had covered.

He was far beyond where he believed the animal could possibly have been when he saw it: a single drop of bright red blood glistening on a shiny gray-green gooseberry leaf. An instant's excitement that his aim had been true gave way to remorse. He had let the deer get away wounded, after all, to suffer and fall victim to some predator.

In a last attempt to locate the buck, Peter set up a stick beside the telltale drop of blood, then backtracked the deer to where it had been lying. Turning around once more, the boy sighted up the hill in a straight line from where he stood, past the marker stick . . . and saw the deer.

It had made perhaps two more jumps during the time when Peter's attention was distracted by the plunging horse, and then it had come to rest in the crevice formed by a slivered chunk of the granite boulder.

Peter walked slowly up to the carcass, thinking about what he must do next. He could not carry the entire deer back to camp, but he could manage to take a hindquarter back with him. Perhaps there was even some way he could use the broken reins to hoist the remaining meat up out of the reach of scavengers until it could be retrieved later.

Standing over the buck, Peter was mentally preparing himself for the gutting and cleaning that must come next in order that the meat would not spoil. He knelt over his boot top to withdraw the hunting knife he carried there.

When he stooped to draw the blade, he heard the tiniest whisper of a sound, directly over his head. Peter's head snapped up and he found himself looking into the pale, amber eyes of a mountain lion. His direct gaze caught the big cat just before springing. The cougar regarded him from near the top of the boulder, where it lay in the shadow of a rocky ledge, and snarled . . . not a scream or ear-splitting roar, but a low, menacing rumble that ended with a coughing sound.

The cougar snarled again, louder this time, and flashed a threatening glimpse of spiked fangs. Peter understood the lion's anger. It had not been on the rock above the brush-choked ravine by chance; no, it too had been stalking the buck until Peter had stolen the kill. But the lion did not intend to part with his meal without a fight.

Very slowly and deliberately, Peter stood erect and began backing away from the base of the boulder. He recalled what he had been taught about never turning his back on a lion. Cougars hunt by stealth and surprise and will attack even humans from behind, given the opportunity. The boy placed each step carefully. He did not want to glance away from the mountain lion, not even for an instant, but he could not risk tangling his foot in the brush and taking a tumble, either. Peter remembered the *Leatherstocking Tales* read to him by his mother; it seemed that Cooper's characters were always falling down when pursued, and Peter did not want this to happen to him.

The lion shifted on its perch and stretched out a great paw toward the deer carcass in an unspoken statement of claim. Then as if reaching a decision, the great cat jumped lightly down from the boulder. It looked once over its shoulder at the dead deer, then fixed its yellow gaze on Peter and began moving slowly toward him.

The boy had backed up about halfway across the brushy slope when he found himself against a tangled gooseberry thicket so dense that he could not push through it. The lion was still padding toward him, but Peter could not risk turning to look for a path across. Instead, he began to move sideways, crablike, hoping to come to a clearer place where he could resume his getaway.

A crashing of branches from the upslope direction drew the attention of both the lion and the boy. A light breeze was blowing up the little draw, or the cougar might have scented the second intruder sooner, but there was no mistake now. Ambling across the brush piles and smashing them down with total disregard for the thorns was a large sow grizzly with a very small cub alongside.

The bear was evidently following the blood smell from the buck, for she was moving with purpose directly toward the carcass, pausing only to sniff the air and correct her course. The lion lashed out an angry snarl that ripped through the morning stillness like a saw blade through lumber.

Giving a wuff of alarm and swatting the cub to get it back behind her, the grizzly stood upright on her hind legs. She shook her massive head and peered around through squinted eyes, the very picture of a myopic matron refusing to take any nonsense.

Peter looked around with alarm. There were no trees to climb near enough that the bear would not be able to reach him first. In fact, the only place of safety close by was the granite monolith, and the lion stood between him and the rock. Peter crouched down right where he was and hoped that he would escape the humpbacked bear's attention.

So far the plan seemed to be working. The mother and cub were still zeroed in on the scent of the deer, and the lion demanded the grizzly's notice by letting loose another full-throated scream. The mother bear snarled and growled in reply, and dropped to all fours again to charge.

The lion jumped back toward the rock ahead of the grizzly's rush and grabbed up the deer by the hind leg. The cat tried to drag the carcass away, but the antlers wedged in the crevice of the rock and would not budge.

The bear charged up with a bellowing roar and swung a paw at the lion in a blow that would have crushed the cougar if it had connected. At the last possible instant, the cat gave up its hold on the deer leg and leaped over the fractured chunk of rock. The two opponents glared and snarled at each other, no farther apart than the width of a tabletop. The lion's ears were flattened against its skull, and it roared and hissed its defiance of the bear.

Peter began to back away again from the scene. He would have no better opportunity than right now to make himself scarce. The grizzly had grasped the deer, her superior weight drawing it free of the crack in the rock where the lion had failed. The cat snarled and slashed and threatened, but the bear, unperturbed, was bent on drawing in the prize.

The boy might have been able to withdraw from the confrontation had it not been for the curiosity of the bear cub. Since Mama had forced the cub to stay back out of harm's way, he had cast around and come across Peter's scent. The grizzly cub shuffled and sniffed his way over the bushes, directly toward the retreating boy. Peter stumbled into a heap of dried gooseberry brambles that crackled underfoot. As if suddenly noticing the absence of her baby, the mother bear whirled around with the mangled body of the deer hanging limply from her jaws.

The rush of the grizzly toward Peter made her earlier charge toward the lion look like a peaceful stroll. With the momentum of an avalanche she galloped across the mesa, her mouth full of venison, bellowing all the while for the cub to get out of the way.

Peter was certain that this was his finish; then, out of the corner of his eye, he saw a streak of tawny lightning. The lion had given up the idea of trying to retrieve the buck, but it was not going to leave empty-handed either. The bear cub squalled as the mountain lion's fangs closed around his neck, and the cougar went bounding away up the slope.

The charging grizzly stopped abruptly and skidded into a sudden turn, reversing direction. In her distress at this new development, she dropped the deer carcass from her grasp and tore off across the mesa in pursuit of the cougar and the stolen cub.

CHAPTER 9

"Whew," muttered Peter, wiping his face with his mascada. "A deer, a lion, *and* a grizzly. It is true, what Paco says, 'Cuando Dios da . . .' when God gives, He gives with a full hand!"

The deer carcass looked to be too mangled and chewed to be worth bothering with. The order of business now was to rejoin the herd and relocate the missing colt—with the saddle still intact, he hoped.

Peter started back across the mesa, pushing aside the coyote brush and retracing the spidery line of the trail. In a hundred yards, a thought struck him and he stopped to consider.

By now the herd was probably already on the move, going farther up the canyon toward the high pastures. If he followed his own trail back, he would come in way behind the location of the next night's camp. This plan would have been reasonable on horseback, since a mounted man can travel farther and faster than a drifting herd of cattle. But on foot, that was another matter altogether.

Peter decided that an angle toward the northeast would cut into the canyon of the jornada. Trail drives are noisy, dusty affairs with slapping leather and plumes of airborne dirt. Once striking the correct arroyo, Peter believed that he would have no difficulty locating the camp.

Taking his bearings, Peter turned so that the sun stood just ahead of his right shoulder; then he started up the slope. He picked out a peak on the horizon that was directly in line with his nose and began hiking.

It was still before noon, but the air was already shimmery with the heat. Cicadas singing in the brush stopped when Peter's shadow passed over them and then resumed their buzzing when he trudged on.

The broken and useless rifle slung over his shoulder was a weight he would gladly have traded for a canteen of water, but he knew better than to leave it behind. A couple hours' walk that was all. With a little luck, the story of his encounter with la osa and señor puma just might protect him from punishment. He hoped so; to a young caballero, the reception he would get arriving in camp on foot was going to be punishment enough.

The canyon that appeared over the next ridge when Peter crossed it was narrow and deep. It had no stream of water flowing in its rocky depths and so could not be the one the herd was following.

By now the sun was directly overhead and it was impossible for Peter to set his course by it. He concluded that it did not really matter, since he had to cross the barranca anyway, and certainly would find the right canyon just over the next ridge.

But the next ridgeline revealed only another narrow, dry arroyo, clearly still not the right one. Worse, while Peter could descend into the canyon, climbing out again up the near vertical wall on the opposite side was not possible. He would have to follow the canyon farther up to locate a way out of the steep embankment.

Walking through the age-old sand of the dry wash, Peter found himself following a looping path. Flash floods had carved the deep canyon, but in slicing through the sandstone layers they had gone around other, harder material, turning the stream bed into a tortuous serpentine. Far above him, through gaps too high to reach, Peter could see towering sandstone columns sculpted by the wind into strange, wavy sentinels.

Peter wondered how far off course he must be. This forbidding landscape did not have the appearance of pasture land. The wall on his right by which he had descended into the canyon dropped lower and lower as he paced along. The bank receded to a low berm, and the hills on that side retreated as the width of the canyon expanded into a small valley. Peter continued hiking, almost oblivious to the newly flat terrain on that side, for his attention was focused on the north.

In fact, his decision to climb out of the flood water's path was not made because he thought of reversing his course but because he hoped to get a wider perspective of the barrier he faced.

Over the bank of the dry stream bed at last, Peter found himself on a level plain covered with small gray-green brush. The flat stretched away to the south and east until it merged with the hazy brown and yellow streaks that were the vague outline of distant hills.

The low bushes crushed when he walked over them, giving off a sharp pungent aroma, not unpleasant, but penetrating. *Sage*, he thought, *like Mother uses in the kitchen*.

The boy now knew that he had completely missed his rendezvous with the herd. He had somehow overshot the mark and would have no choice but to back-track his own trail. But a greater concern came first. Peter recognized that he needed water—and soon. The way back was a long distance to a stream.

Up ahead, a line of alamos, cottonwoods, presented the possibility of moisture. If not a pool, perhaps at least a spring. Peter changed his direction to line up directly with the little clump of trees.

For a long time, Peter trudged across the sage-covered field without looking up. He amused himself by watching his shadow flow over the brush and mount the ground-squirrel mounds as it marched along ahead of him.

The boy was not alarmed at his predicament. The nights were not cold enough for the lack of a fire to be a problem, and tomorrow he could retrace his steps. He regretted having refused Paco's advice; he wished now he had eaten breakfast. Still, water was the pressing issue. Tomorrow he would meet up with someone looking for him and then there would be food.

Glancing up from his shadow and his thoughts, Peter corrected his course slightly and checked his progress toward the cottonwoods.

The dark dots on the horizon grew into tree shapes. The images wavered with the heat waves reflected off the red soil. The upper half of each tree appeared to be floating, while the lower half had disappeared.

Floating alongside the trees were two brown dome-like bodies that hovered above the ground. Peter stared and squinted, trying to determine exactly what he was seeing. In appearance, the forms were like two extremely large brown bears, sleeping near the line of trees.

The recent experience with the bear and the lion made the boy cautious. If there was water near the cottonwoods, then it could very well be a place where grizzlies came to drink.

Peter stood inspecting the shapes, then advanced a little and studied them again. A change in the light and shadow revealed a third domed shape and then a fourth and a fifth. Understanding flooded Peter's mind, but he did not know whether to be relieved or more anxious. The group of rounded images shimmering in the afternoon sun were huts—the dwellings of a tribe of what Peter called the Wild Ones . . . Indians.

———

There was no turning back. Peter needed water and he needed it now. That an Indian rancheria existed by the line of cottonwoods meant a certainty of finding water, and Peter meant to have it.

The dome-shaped huts grew in his vision and increased in number as he got closer. They were oddly placed in irregular groups. Peter was curious as to why he saw no people out and about. The afternoon was wearing on, but it was not late enough or cool enough for the people to stay indoors. *Perhaps this is a deserted village,* Peter thought. *I hope they didn't leave because the water ran out.*

No dogs barked at his approach, no horses stamped, no children played, no adults watched him, and yet . . . Peter had the eerie feeling that the village, though clearly deserted, had only recently been abandoned.

At the edge of the cleared ground that marked the collection of huts, the village was tucked into a fold of hillside where a rockfall released a spring. There was not enough water to run down the creek bed, but there was a trickle of the precious liquid that dripped steadily down from the ledges and filled a good-sized pool. The overflow of the pond made its way downstream only a few yards before it was swallowed by the thirsty sand. It was barely enough to supply a village of this size and keep the cottonwoods alive as well. Perhaps the people *had* moved on.

Peter went directly to the spring. He eyed the stagnant basin with its covering of yellow-green scum, and then turned to the rocky ledge. Cupping his hands beneath the seep, Peter waited patiently for a handful of water to drip into his grasp. He drank it greedily, waited for his palms to refill, and drank again.

His eyes glanced downward as he waited for his hands to fill the third time. At first nothing seemed out of the ordinary, but then his mind focused on what his eyes saw: There was a footprint directly under the drip of the spring. In the sandy verge of the pool was the imprint of five large naked toes.

Staring at his own feet, encased in soft leather boots, Peter came to the inescapable conclusion. Not only was there at least one other person around the camp, but the dripping water would have obliterated the track in no more than ten or fifteen minutes. Whoever it was could not be far away.

Peter tried to backtrack the trail, but other footprints could not be seen. Beyond the line of the alamo trees, a dust devil danced and hopped its way over the sage. The dry, thin dirt would not hold a track long against the sweeping breeze, except in a sheltered place such as near the rocks.

The way the wind swished through the camp, there

was no true lee side to be sheltered, and no more distinct prints met Peter's eye. He circled one hut, then another and a third without finding any evidence of another human.

"Hola," he called. "Is anybody here?" There was no answer but the rustle of the cottonwood leaves. Discarded baskets and tools lay scattered about. An odor of decay assaulted Peter's nose, and he did not enter any of the buildings.

Next to the third deserted hovel was a circular heap of rubble where a hut had burned to the ground. Most of the ashes had been blown away by the wind, but fragments of charred timber remained. Peter studied the location for a moment, then went past another abandoned structure, which also had a burned-out hulk beside it.

He passed another hut, buzzing with a cloud of flies, and then two more burned spaces. The boy thought how strange it was for the village to suffer so many fires, and yet not lose *all* the buildings. He stood beside a fifth burned place and examined the debris. A broken clay pot was overturned in the center of the rubble. Peter idly kicked at the shard with his toe.

The pot fragment rolled over to reveal a human skull. Its empty eye sockets stared up at Peter, and even without the lower jaw there seemed to be a malicious grin to its expression.

Peter ran toward the edge of the camp, passing standing huts and burned-out ruins without looking. He did not stop running until he was beyond the last of the domed houses and was outside the village next to a long, low mound of earth.

He forced himself to stop; his breath was coming in

ragged gasps and his heart was pounding in his ears. What was he afraid of? Old dead bones could not hurt anyone, nor was Peter a child to be frightened anymore by Paco's ghost stories about headless vaqueros and haunted caves.

He dropped down on the mound next to a discarded deer hide to rest and think, to regain the composure that he thought an almost-adult should have. He laid down the broken gun and reviewed the situation: some disaster had hit this village, with multiple fires that had claimed at least one victim. Also, as lately as a few minutes before his arrival, there had been some person—not a ghost but a living, barefoot human—walking in the camp. *Now what?* he thought.

As if in answer to his unspoken question, the earth beneath him moaned. Not a quick groaning sound like Peter had heard when tree limbs rub together in a wind storm, but a long, drawn-out sigh of misery.

Peter jumped up from the mound. From the highest part of the long barrow of earth, near its center, a puff of smoke drifted up. At the same time, the deer hide lying on the ground stirred and shook as if something were coming out. *The demon caballero riding forth!*

Adult composure or not, Peter was *not* remaining to see what actually came out of the ground. He was already up and running back toward the spring when he remembered the rifle.

It was a credit to Peter's discipline, if not his courage, that he turned around and raced back to reclaim the gun. He had just reached it when the deer hide shook itself free of some clods of earth that had rolled down on it and it flipped open to reveal a tunnel into the mound. Peter stood transfixed as a small bony hand was followed by a sleeve of coarse gray cloth and then the familiar small form of . . .

"Father Francis!" Peter cried with relief. "What are you doing here? And what is this place? Where is everybody?"

The priest was just as dumbfounded as the boy. "Don Peter," he said, brushing off his robe and standing up to look around. "Is your father here?" His face was lined and drawn and his expression anxious.

In a few clipped phrases, Peter explained how he came to be lost and wander into the village. The priest then shook his head with a sorrowful expression. "You cannot remain here, Peter. It may cost you your life."

"Why? What is it?"

"Smallpox," came the weary, toneless answer. "The village is dying."

Father Francis had only a few moments in which to explain about the village and its desperate condition. "I alone am able to care for the people calling for water in their dreadful fevers."

Only a month earlier the village had been thriving. Bustling with the summer activities of preparing hides and gathering chia seeds for meal, the Yokuts had welcomed a group of twenty British sailors who said they had come to settle.

Always hospitable, the Yokuts noted that the sailors were sickly and weak and many exhibited small sores and pock marks. The Indian elders had done what they could to supply the needs of the newcomers and treated them with such medicine as was known.

Two weeks later, the first of the Yokuts fell ill. The next day two more and the following day six. The traditional Yokut ceremony of burning the bodies of the dead inside their huts with all their belongings had been carried out at a pace that accelerated daily. What prevented the rancheria from being totally reduced to ashes was only that no people remained who were strong enough to carry out the cremations. Only Father Francis was untouched by the disease, and he was too busy caring for the sick and dying to bother with the dead, now piled in two of the remaining huts.

"Only two of the Britishers died," Father Francis said, "but the rest fled—back to their ships, I suppose."

"But why have all the sick people gone into the hole in the ground?"

"It is our way," Father Francis replied. "The sweat lodge has always been our cure for sickness, and now all who are left alive have gone there."

Peter looked around at the dusty valley and the slight frame of the careworn priest. "You need help," the boy said. "I will stay to aid you."

"God bless you, my son," Father Francis said sincerely. His body swayed as he made the sign of the cross. "But it cannot be. I will not risk your life—" He stopped suddenly and said, "Perhaps God has sent you here for a greater purpose than you can know." The priest retreated abruptly into the bowels of the earth.

When he emerged again a moment later, he had a tiny bundle, wrapped in doeskin. Father Francis stood before Peter, who watched curiously as the priest tucked back a fold of soft white hide to reveal the face of a baby.

"His name is Limik—*Falcon*, the same as my grandfather," Father Francis said. "He is only two days old. My cousin's baby."

"But his mother?" asked Peter.

The priest shook his head sadly. "She will not live another night. I despaired of keeping this little one alive, but now I see that heaven has sent you for that reason."

Peter drew back sharply. "Me?" he asked incredulously. "You want *me* to care for this baby?"

A strand of fluff from a cottonwood tree drifted down out of the sky and landed across the baby's nose. Impulsively, Peter reached over to pluck the strand away. Limik, who had been gnawing on his fist, opened his hand and grasped Peter's little finger in a grip surprisingly strong.

The young ranchero gulped. "All right," he said. "What do I do?"

———

The lines of white surf had already disappeared and the red tile roofs and whitewashed adobe walls were fading into the backdrop of dusty green California hills as the *Juno* stood away from Santa Barbara.

Father McNamara and Captain Blake stood and regarded the receding shoreline. Blake said gloomily, "I do not relish having to report to Admiral Seymour on the complete failure of our mission here."

Father McNamara was more sanguine. "Tut, Captain," he said, "it is not your fault that events proceeded so rapidly. Who would have foreseen that the Americans would be prepared enough to achieve their seizure of San Francisco, San Diego, and Monterey, all within one month? They will be lounging about the Pueblo of Los Angeles and wandering through Santa Barbara in another week."

"But the scheme to colonize!" Blake exclaimed,

dashing his fist against the taffrail. "It should have worked!"

"Yes. It is a pity that your sailors were not able to perform as expected. But let me cheer you up with another plan which I expect to lay before Admiral Seymour."

"What might that be?"

"Ah, a capital scheme to be sure . . . controlling the crossroads of the Pacific, I call it. Tell me, Captain, have you ever been to the Sandwich Islands, discovered by the inestimable Captain Cook? I believe in the native tongue the land is called Ohwyhee. . . ."

CHAPTER 10

The boom of the twelve-inch cannon echoed around the Santa Barbara roadstead. The arrival signal rolled past the mission, up San Marcos Pass, and back again. The report reverberated in the ears of Nicholas Den as he sat in his counting house. The curly-haired Irish ranchero was reviewing columns of figures for "California bank notes." Each entry represented cowhides worth two dollars, American. "What ship can that be?" he muttered to himself. "Julio," he called to his Indian servant, "fetch my telescope."

Den's eyes crinkled at the corners in the pleasant anticipation of some trading to be done. He climbed the stairs to the flat roof of his office two steps at a time. "Could it be the *Juno* back from Monterey in only a week?" he thought aloud. "If it is, they'll be wanting twenty head or so for meat."

"Don Nicholas," said Julio, handing him the spyglass, "I do not recognize this ship. She is a frigate, sí?"

"Not so fast," corrected Nicholas Den, snapping open the brass telescope and fitting it to his eyes. "We'll know in a moment. She must be one of Admiral Seymour's—" He let out a gasp. "That's not a British ship— they're flying the Stars and Stripes . . . she's American!"

The word spread quickly through the settlement and into the countryside beyond, bringing a crowd of curious onlookers to the beach.

"Can you make out the name of the vessel?" someone asked Don Nicholas.

"She's swinging around now . . . yes," he said, "the *Congress.*"

The small boat being rowed ashore from the frigate looked to be in danger of swamping. Besides the six sailors manning the oars, there were ten men carrying muskets with the muzzles held rigidly upright.

As the boat swept onto the sand, two of the sailors jumped overboard to guide the boat farther on the shore. When the little vessel was beached, it was dragged up past the high watermark, and only then did its distinguished-looking passenger get out.

The man who stepped out of the boat onto the Santa Barbara landing was no taller than Don Nicholas and thinner of face and body. He was wearing the full dress uniform of a commodore of the United States Navy. Despite the warm summer temperature, every brass button of his double-breasted coat was secured, right up to the high, stiff collar worked with gold. His gold epaulets glinted and gleamed in the sunlight as he proceeded directly to where Don Nicholas stood.

"Sir," he said formally in English, "I am seeking the alcalde of this place, Don Nicholas Den. Can you help me locate him?"

"It depends," Don Nicholas replied, shifting uncomfortably. "What do you want him for?"

"Why, to announce my arrival and give him my compliments," the youthful-looking man with the aristocratic nose said with a touch of sarcasm. "No matter . . . I have other pressing business. Mr. Mitchell, if you please."

"Fall in!" commanded a midshipman in a high, nervous treble.

Leaving the sailors beside the boat, a double file of marines escorted the naval commander and midshipmen up away from the beach. The crowd of curious Barbareños followed, but at a respectful distance. After all, the soldiers' muskets were fixed with bayonets, and their field packs and grim expressions suggested that they meant business.

The main thoroughfare of Santa Barbara was little more than a muddy track more suited to carreta oxcarts than to precise military formations. The Americanos knew exactly where they were going, however, and stepped out smartly, even when they had to wade across Mission Creek.

The formation followed the rutted highway directly to the old adobe presidio. There were no Mexican soldiers present, since the remaining few guards had been withdrawn when Governor Pico had retreated to Los Angeles only a few days before.

The courtyard was empty except for a forgotten goat and a flock of chickens pecking in the dirt. The whole fort had an air of dilapidation and abandonment. The slumping adobe walls could have been deserted for a century instead of just a week.

The commodore looked around uncertainly, as if wondering how to demand the surrender of a town when there was no opposition. "Mr. Mitchell," he said at last, "I'll have our flag run up the flagpole, if you please."

"Begging your pardon, sir," apologized the middie. "But there is no flagpole, sir."

The young American officer tugged on his bushy sideburns and frowned. "All right, then," he concluded, "we'll just march until we find one!"

After slogging down narrow lanes even more rutted than the main highway, the detachment of troops came to a halt in front of a two-story adobe casa. It looked like many other nondescript tan brick buildings in Santa Barbara, with one notable exception: it had a flagpole. The slender mast was actually a semaphore staff that its owner, Don Nicholas Den, kept to exchange signal flag greetings with ships in the harbor, but it would do.

"Mr. Mitchell, you will post the colors," ordered the commodore.

The middie saluted sharply and called the detail to attention. The red, white, and blue of Old Glory was soon hoisted to the peak.

Much whispered commentary erupted from the crowd and Don Nicholas stepped forward in protest. "Sir," he said stiffly, "what do you think you are doing?"

"Well, señor alcalde, mayor. You *are* Nicholas Den, aren't you?" inquired the commodore.

Don Nicholas stumbled back a pace. "How did you—"

The naval officer brushed the question aside in favor of answering the earlier challenge. "I am Commodore Stockton of the United States Navy. Inasmuch as the United States and the country of Mexico are now at war, I am hereby taking possession of the Santa Barbara presidial district."

As soon as the word of Commodore Stockton's invasion reached the Reed Rancho, Francesca ordered her gray Barileno mare saddled, and she set off for town. No word had come from Will, nor news about him. But he had gone seeking Americans, and it was to the Americans that she would go for information.

Stockton had set up his headquarters in Nicholas Den's office and was proceeding to treat Santa Barbara as conquered territory. Francesca was stopped by a sentry outside Don Nicholas's doorway, but that did not prevent her from overhearing the conversation within. "And I expect you, Don Nicholas," a high-pitched, nasal voice was saying, "to be responsible for keeping the peace. I will be departing shortly to continue the campaign, but I will leave Midshipman Mitchell and Lieutenant Falls, along with a platoon of marines."

"Commodore," an unhappy-sounding Don Nicholas sputtered, "I must protest! How can you force me, a Mexican citizen, to administer the laws of a foreign invader? It is against all the rules of the civilized world!"

"Civilized world be hanged!" the nasal voice retorted. "I intend to see that order is maintained in Santa Barbara, by force if necessary. If you wish such an unfortunate consequence to be avoided, you will do your utmost to make certain that the citizenry remain cooperative and peaceable." The finality of both words and tone left no doubt in Francesca's mind that she had just heard the last pronouncement on the subject. "Now," the voice continued in a quiet volume, "as to quarters for my men. Your own rancho, Dos Pueblos, is just outside of town. Is that correct?" A short man in a crisp blue uniform paced in front of the doorway.

Don Nicholas sputtered again and choked. His bulging eyes and beet-red face gave a good imitation of a man suffering apoplexy. But he was saved from responding by a marine guard announcing that a lady wished to speak with Commodore Stockton.

The officer spun on his heel to face Francesca. The words that he did not wish to be disturbed were on his lips, but Francesca watched him check himself and saw his gaze inspect her face and figure. Striking a military pose with one hand behind his back and the other grasping his jacket lapel, the banty rooster of a man addressed her. "What may I do for you, señora?"

Seizing on the interruption, Don Nicholas said smoothly, "May I present Doña Francesca? Her husband is an American, and their rancho is even closer to Santa Barbara and more spacious than my own humble casa."

"Wonderful," said Stockton, eyeing Francesca. "Your husband is American? Where is he? Is he in favor of our, uh, activities?"

Francesca fixed the commodore with a steady gaze of her dark eyes. "It is about my husband that I have come to see you, sir," she said. "My husband, Don Will Reed, went north some time ago to inquire into the reported deaths of our godchildren, Ramon and Carlos Carrillo. I have not heard from him since. Do you know his whereabouts, or if he made contact with the American commander named Fremont?"

Stockton's face grew grim. "I know something of the death of the Carrillos," he said. "I must tell you, madam, that they were executed as spies, and if your husband had any connection—"

"They were *not* spies!" Francesca snapped, her eyes flashing. "They were barely older than my own son! And what of my husband? Do you know of him?"

"Know *of* him? Yes, I know of him . . . he attacked Captain Fremont's landing party in Yerba Buena. He is a prisoner, madam, and after trial will face further imprisonment—or worse."

Francesca's already pale skin turned ashen, and she groped for the office chair into which Don Nicholas guided her. "You cannot mean it," she murmured, shaking her head. "It cannot be so."

Stockton looked stern. "Don Nicholas," he said with finality, "under the circumstances, I think it entirely appropriate to adopt your suggestion. Lieutenant Falls and half the troops will be billeted at the Reed rancho."

Staring at the wood-planked floor, Francesca bit her lip and held a lace handkerchief to her eyes. She said nothing at the outrage and barely heard Don Nicholas inquire, "And the rest?"

"I think that some should remain closer to the center of the town. Yes, I'd say the remaining troops can bivouac right here in your office building."

———

"They are thieves and cutthroats, these Americanos," declared Simona, the cook in the Reed household. With one infant on her hip and a toddler trailing after, Simona helped Francesca stash the most precious household belongings into a large trunk. Luis, her diminutive vaquero husband, was already hard at work digging a hole in the floor of the stall reserved for the master's horse, Flotada.

126

Silver table service, tea sets, goblets, and candelabra were wrapped in delicate lace and linens. All the weapons, including table knives, were placed into the trunk lest the Americanos carry out their threat to arrest every citizen caught with a weapon of any kind.

Her face grim, Francesca warned Simona, "Tell Luis that these Americanos are greatly afraid of vaqueros. They know how accomplished our men are with their reatas, and now have made the rule that anyone with a reata will be publicly whipped or arrested. We will bury the reatas in the trunk as well."

"They are loco!" fumed Simona as she hurried out the door. "If Don Will were here, they would not treat us like prisoners."

Francesca was secretly relieved that Will was not here, even if it meant he was in jail. Certainly he would not stand for the endless list of regulations that the American Lieutenant Falls had imposed upon the "conquered" people:

BY ORDER OF THE AMERICAN
COMMANDER LT. FALLS
1. Shops will be closed at sundown
2. No alcohol will be sold
3. A strict 10 P.M. curfew will be enforced
4. No meetings to be held
5. No two people may be on the street together
6. No assembly of more than two people
7. No carrying of firearms
8. No carrying of reatas or tailing of steers

American Commander Lt. Falls will act as civil judge in the absence of Commodore Stockton. All violations of the above regulations are punishable by whippings, imprisonment, or death. Houses may be searched if a suspicion of wrong-doing exists.

The scrawny, arrogant Lieutenant Falls had dictated his rules as he paced back and forth on the porch of city hall. Written in English and posted on the wall of every shop and home in Santa Barbara, the regulations were then read aloud in Spanish from the rooftops. Clusters of astonished citizens had listened, then looked at one another in the realization that anyone standing among a group of three or more could instantly be arrested and punished.

The crowd had simply evaporated. No doubt every Santa Barbara resident had hurried home to do the same thing Francesca was doing now. Every valuable would have to be hidden. The new laws were not laws meant to protect from harm. They were simply designed to grant absolute power to the strutting little tyrant who would soon be moving into Francesca's own home.

Simona returned with the reatas, which she wrapped in a sheet and placed at the top of the chest. "Luis says he understands why the Americanos fear our skill with the reata," she said to Francesca. "But why have they made a law against the tailing of steers?" She shook her head at the madness of such a proclamation.

Francesca laughed a short, bitter laugh. "Perhaps these Americano cows have tails beneath their uniforms. Perhaps they have seen the way our vaqueros can flip a steer by simply cranking its tail. No doubt this Lieutenant Falls is afraid Luis will crank the man's tail and he will live up to his American name."

That explanation was as reasonable as any, since the whole list seemed to border on insanity.

"Don Reed would tail this strutting calf if he were home! Did you see him parade around as though he were some handsome mayordomo on a prancing stallion? His teeth poking out from those thick lips! And he has only half his hair. Skinny neck and a pot belly, too! A very poor specimen of Americano, if you ask me. It is a good thing we know Don Reed, or we could think them all piggish and pitiful and . . . *loco*!" She finished where the conversation had begun.

"If he is loco, then perhaps he is also very dangerous, Simona." Francesca closed the trunk and snapped the lock closed. "I have heard my father speak of men such as this Lieutenant Falls before. He sees danger in every look and believes that each whispered word is about himself. He feels that he is much despised—"

"And so he is!"

"Ah, but he does not believe that such hatred is justified. His whole existence depends on fighting some personal enemy. For this reason, men like Falls work very hard at making enemies of all men. It is a twisted mind. A twisted and dangerous life." Francesca glanced worriedly out the window. "We must be careful, Simona. He has made himself the law. If we offend him, we are subject to his revenge."

"The fact that we were here first offends him."

"Think of your children. Smile and keep silent until someone sane returns to put an end to this madness." She was glad that Peter was in the hills, relieved that Will was far beyond the reach of this little madman. She would pray for Will's release and safe return, but not if homecoming meant greater danger!

The company of eight marines rode toward the Reed rancho as Francesca and Simona stood on the porch. Luis hurriedly spread straw to cover the turned earth in Flotada's stall.

On the shoulder and rump of every horse, Francesca recognized the brands of the finest ranchos in the country. She was justified in burying her belongings. These vile men took what they wanted.

Simona noticed the brands at the same moment. Through gritted teeth the plump cook declared, "Thieves and cutthroats, señora Reed. They should be riding wild burros! American pigs!"

"Whatever you say," Francesca reminded her, "say it with a sweet smile. They do not speak our language, Simona, but this Lieutenant Falls fancies himself to be both judge and lawgiver. No doubt he studies the expression on our faces even now." She raised her chin slightly and smiled like a gentlewoman welcoming guests to the hacienda—no trace of the bitter resentment of this violation . . . not a hint of the disdain she felt for the pitiful little Americano lieutenant. He flapped awkwardly against the saddle and tugged at the reins of the magnificent horse he rode.

"It is pathetic to see when the horse is finer than the one on his back," said Simona in Spanish. Her face was also a reflection of genuine hospitality as the riders approached.

"The horse should be riding señor Falls, I think," agreed Francesca. "The animal knows more than the man in this case."

The eight marines pulled their mounts to a halt before the porch. Francesca and Simona both curtsied in unison.

"Good afternoon, madam," said a breathless Falls as his nervous horse pranced about the yard and fought the harsh tugging on the bit. "You have prepared for us?"

"Welcome to the Reed Rancho, Lieutenant," Francesca said graciously. "I have moved my belongings to the servant quarters. You and your men are welcome here. My husband, who is an American also, will be pleased that you have chosen our home to reside in during your stay."

"Your English is quite good," said Falls, jerking the horse around in a tight circle. "I will thank you to speak only English in the presence of me and my men at all times."

"But my servants do not speak your language, señor Falls. What if I must speak to them in front of you?"

"Well then . . . you will provide us with a proper English translation in such a case. We cannot have you Mexicans conniving behind our backs, can we?"

With a gracious nod, Francesca agreed. "As you wish, señor."

"And I am not a *señor*. I am no Mexican, madam, but an American officer."

Again the nod. Then Simona asked in Spanish, "What does this *cabro* say, Doña Reed?" She continued to smile demurely at the officer, who was unaware that cabro meant *goat*.

"May I explain to my servant what you have just told me?" Francesca asked.

"Tell her," Falls ordered.

Francesca did so in Spanish. "The cabro says that I

am to speak only English to him and give him the translation of every Spanish word uttered in his presence."

"Sí," agreed Simona with a nod at the American. There was no change in her expression. "Caporal de cabestros." Simona uttered the salute, *Captain of Oxen*, with respect.

"What did she say?" Falls demanded.

"She calls you Captain of Horsemen, an honored title," Francesca answered. Indeed, the word for *oxen* was quite close to the word *caballero*, horseman. "Does the title please you, Lieutenant? If so, it is a simple title for my servants to use. Their tongues cannot master the difficulties of your language, I fear."

Yes. He liked it. *Caporal de cabestros*. It had a ring to it.

With a self-satisfied smile, the Captain of Oxen set his muddy boots in the home of Will and Francesca Reed.

CHAPTER 11

Tor Fowler was leading a gray horse as he approached the guard outside the adobe block hut—the same hut in which he had lately been held. Will was now confined there; an iron gate had replaced the wooden door. "Davis," Fowler said, peering at the guard as if in disbelief, "is that you?"

Davis hastily put down a tin plate of beans and wiped grease from his whisker-stubbled chin. "Hello, Fowler," he said nervously. "I heerd you was back."

"Yup," Fowler agreed. "You know that feller in there," he said, pointing to the hut. "He saved my life."

"I heerd something like that," Davis nodded. "But he's a turncoat what's to be sent to Sutter's with the other prisoners."

Fowler nodded and studied Davis's face intently so long that the settler fidgeted, shuffling his feet. "What're you lookin' at, anyhow?" he demanded at last.

"They tell me you was nearly killed, shot in the head, escaping. Same time I got took prisoner. That so?"

The smallest mark remained on Davis's forehead from where the tree limb had batted him to the ground. A twitching hand rubbed over the spot and traced around it as if pretending the wound were larger. "Yup," Davis said at last.

"Got you promoted too?"

Davis bobbed his head. "Corporal of Californie Volunteers," he said, "ever since we took care of them Carrillo assassin fellers." Then as if drawing renewed confidence from remembering his rank, he demanded, "What do you want here, Fowler?"

"Hear that?" Fowler asked, jerking his chin toward the sound of a cannon fire salute. "Captain Montgomery is comin' ashore to read a proclamation. Probably be a regular fiesta after."

"So?" said Davis unhappily. "I got to guard this here prisoner." He hefted an army-issue musket. "And I don't need no help from you."

"Thought you might like to go on down to the party and leave me on guard a spell." Fowler's voice sounded surprised at Davis's hostility. The barest droop of an eyelid over a gray eye was directed at the doorway.

"What kinda danged fool do you take me for? Everybody knows you favor lettin' this fella loose!" A move closer by Fowler made Davis draw the musket up to chest height and cock the hammer back. "That's far enough," he warned.

Fowler held up both empty hands, palms outward. "Whatever are you scared of, Davis?" he said innocently, taking one more pace nearer.

Unconsciously, Davis backed up a step and his shoulders touched the iron gate across the door. "I'm warnin' you," he said, and he raised the musket to his shoulder.

From behind him, Will's hand shot out through the grating and grasped the barrel of the musket. The gun erupted with a roar, striking nothing, its blast blending with the rolling cannon fire. Will yanked back hard on the weapon, pinning the settler by the neck to the metal frame.

Eyes bulging and hands waving frantically, Davis saw Fowler take one more step. He even saw the haymaker that started down by Fowler's side and flashed in an overhand arc toward his nose. Briefly he saw shooting stars, then the settler saw nothing as Will let him slip to the ground.

"That was for Cap McBride and Two Strike," Fowler muttered, rummaging through Davis's pockets and coming out with the key to free Will.

"Thanks," Will offered, emerging into the sunlight. "Now tell me where that fellow Falls has gone, and we're all square."

Fowler shook his head. "I'm still comin' with you," he said. "Nothin' left for me around here. Castro's moved south; Fremont, too. I figure there'll be a fight round Santa Barbara somewheres."

Will started. "My home!" he said. "What about Falls?"

Gray eyes locked on green. "Left by ship," Fowler said. "Fremont sent him ahead to Santa Barbara to cut off Castro's retreat."

A crowd of spectators gathered on the dirt field that passed as Yerba Buena's public square. Russian sailors, whaling men, Frenchmen off a merchant vessel, and American traders all jostled for a better view, but there were few Californios. The Spanish-speaking residents mostly stayed indoors.

Those who stood before the Customs House could see boats being lowered from the United States ship *Potsmouth*. Seventy black-hatted sailors rowed ashore at Clark's Point at one end of the arc of Yerba Buena cove.

To the brittle noise of one drum and the shrill prattle of one fife, the files of men marched to the square. Down came the Mexican Flag, and the Stars and Stripes was hoisted in its place.

But the banner at which a small knot of Californios were staring was neither of these. At the rear of the crowd stood Juan Padilla, flanked by a dozen men. Their wide poblano hat brims were pulled low over their eyes, and under their serapes they held pistols. The flag at which Padilla directed his attention was a white sheet with a red stripe along its bottom edge. The crudely lettered words *California Republic* paralleled the stripe. In the center of the flag was a hulking shape meant to be a grizzly bear.

One of Padilla's friends made an obscene comment and the men laughed, the sound covered by the cheering of the rest of the crowd. "Looks like a cochino prieto, a black *pig*, to me," Padilla added.

"What do we do now, Capitan?" whispered Four Fingers hoarsely. "Do we ride south to aid General Castro?"

Padilla repeated the obscene remark that had been applied to the Bear Flag. "We ride south," he agreed, "but we go only to aid ourselves! Vámanos!"

————

Peter stopped pounding the chia-grass seed long enough to pick up the tiny wailing Limik and rock him for a moment. "Just wait a bit," Peter soothed. "I'll have food for you soon."

He stirred the pounded seeds into a gourd bowl half full of water. Using a pair of wooden tongs, Peter picked up a clean round stone that had been heating by a fire of mesquite wood. He dropped the stone into the bowl of porridge and stirred it until it began to steam.

"You are hungry all the time, Limik," he said, "but that's all right because you will grow up strong." Peter dipped his finger in the porridge, then let the baby suck the thick gruel. Limik wrinkled his face as if to say that the meal was not altogether to his liking, but he continued eating. "I know we need milk, but there is nothing I can do about that now."

Father Francis stumbled out of the sweat lodge. His robes were drenched in perspiration and his brown complexion had turned almost as gray as his robes. He was exhausted.

Stooping beside the trickle of water from the spring, Father Francis splashed a few drops over his own face, then thrust a gourd under the flow to let it fill. When the bowl was nearly full, he turned to go back to his charges, but stopped beside Peter and the baby as if he had just seen them. A weary smile played across his face, and his eyes lightened just a touch. He stretched out his hand as if to place it on the baby's head, then drew it back quickly without contact. "They say this sickness is spread by the touch," he croaked.

Across the plain, up from the canyon, four swirls of dust appeared. At first they seemed to be nothing more than dust devils in some curious parallel flight, but soon they resolved into riders, coming at a hard gallop. Peter pointed them out to Father Francis. The priest shaded his eyes and squinted, then asked, "Can you make them out, my son?"

Covering Limik carefully in his doeskin wrapper, Peter laid the baby down on a hide, then hopped up on a ledge of rock. "The lead rider is on a tall mule," the young ranchero said. "It looks like . . . Paco!"

In a few minutes the Reed mayordomo and two vaqueros rode into the Yokut camp. They had brought Peter's horse, Chino, with them.

"Peter! Hijito, little son! Where have you been?" Paco managed to sound angry and relieved in the same breath. "Your horse wandered in without his rider, and we found not only oso tracks but also puma tracks over yours. Now here you are, miles away from . . . what is that?"

The flow of questions and rebukes ceased abruptly as the thin wail of baby Limik came up from the bundle on the ground. Paco's mule snorted and cross stepped sideways as a small brown arm broke free of its doeskin wrap and waved angrily in the air. "Father Francis," Paco addressed the priest, "where are all the Indios? And how long has Don Peter been here?"

Father Francis waited patiently for the stream of words to subside again before explaining. When he had finished, the two vaqueros had purposely backed their mounts several paces toward the edge of camp and Paco was looking nervous. "So you see," concluded the priest, "Don Peter was sent by God to serve the needs of this little one. And now that you have arrived, Paco, you must take them both back to Santa Barbara at once."

"But what about you?" Peter blurted out. "You alone cannot care for everyone."

The gray robe, once a perfect fit around the sinewy arms and legs of Father Francis, appeared to have grown. The folds of coarse cloth swallowed up the little man. "No," the priest said, "there are very few left now . . . I will manage."

At that moment the cowl slipped backward, exposing the drawn features of Father Francis. And in the hollow of his neck, at the base of his throat, a single yellow dot. The priest saw Peter's stare. "Peter, my son, do you remember what follows the rodeo, the round-up?"

Peter looked surprised at a question that seemed so out of place, but he answered respectfully, "Sí, what follows is de escoger y desechar, the choosing and the discarding."

"Just so," Father Francis agreed. "You and I have both been chosen, Don Peter, but we must go to different fields for a time."

The boy bit his lip. "Will I see you again?" he managed to say.

"Of course," replied Father Francis, smiling once more. "In the Rodeo Grande. Isn't there always a parada de escojidos, a parade of the selected ones? We will be there together, you and I."

A deep saddlebag was emptied of its provisions: jerked beef and small sacks of rice and cornmeal. The pack was lined with rabbit fur, and then baby Limik was carefully tucked inside. The bag was secured to Paco's saddle, and Peter mounted Chino. "I will miss you," the young ranchero said to the priest.

"Vayan con Dios," Father Francis said softly. "Go with God."

It was inevitable that the American officer Falls would become the object of quiet ridicule on the Reed Rancho as well as in the town of Santa Barbara. Greeted by young and old alike as *el cabro*, the goat, the salute was always uttered in such a respectful tone that the little tyrant did not catch on. He was told, and believed, that cabro meant *leader*.

"*Buenos días, el cabro*," said priest and mission Indian and schoolchild alike. *Good day, you goat.*

He always nodded his too-large head in acknowledgment, although he did not speak. Later, he ordered Francesca to let it be known that he liked this title better than the one which meant Captain of Horsemen because it was shorter and easier for him to keep track of. Too many Spanish words made him uncomfortable, even when those words were meant to convey his authority of the community of Barbareños.

This small conspiracy among the citizens somehow helped to ease the tension of the almost intolerable oppression. When a runaway steer tore through the main street of Santa Barbara and was halted when a vaquero tailed it to the ground, *el cabro* Falls carried out his threat and had the vaquero publicly whipped. From windows and doorways, citizens watched the whipping with hostile eyes. Forbidden to gather together for solace or action against such injustice, they comforted themselves by smiling and greeting *el cabro* at every opportunity.

Each new outrage was met with this quiet inner resistance. Not every Americano could be so loco! After all, señor Reed was a kind and good man. Certainly this Lieutenant Falls was some sort of aberration, a *diablero*, a demonic lunatic who would sink back to hell before the summer was past.

He added the proclamation that there would be no church services. Visits to the mission were restricted to one worshiper at a time. The citizens complied, entering the sanctuary one person at a time, lighting candles one at a time, until all the prayers and all the candles added up to one great hope—that soon the oppression of *el cabro* would be lifted from the tiny village.

CHAPTER 12

It was late when Peter and Paco rode into the syc-amore-bordered lane that led up to Casa Reed. The two vaqueros had accompanied the young ranchero and his mayordomo only as far as the mouth of the canyon before turning back to rejoin the herd.

Baby Limik was sleeping in his makeshift cradle. Fed not an hour before on a mixture of chia gruel and cow's milk, he was happily sucking his thumb and being rocked by the gentle motion of the mule.

"Wait a moment," requested Paco, gesturing for Peter to stop. "I must walk a bit or my leg will stiffen completely."

"I thought you said vaqueros were too tough to notice a little thing like a kick in the shins," Peter teased.

Paco was not amused. "Next time, *I* will mind the reatas and *you* may milk the wild cow! Caramba! That hurts!"

"It was all for a good cause; and anyway, there won't be a next time. Mother will know of someone to nurse the child, probably tonight. *If*," he added with empha-sis, "we don't dawdle too long in getting home."

Remounting the mule, Paco said, "You know, young Pedrito, you have a cruel streak about you." Then the mayordomo leaned over to check the slumbering infant. Peter could not see the tenderness that crept across the Indian vaquero's weathered face, but he could hear the man's gruff voice soften when he said, "We must take good care of him, Don Pedro. He is our godchild, you know. Perhaps the last of all his people."

Peter shuddered at the remembrance of the terrible loneliness and the stench of death that clung to the Yokut village. "Come along then," he said with fervor, "let's get home."

The lights of Peter's house had just come into view around a bend in the lane when a voice from the darkness ordered in English, "Halt! Who goes there?"

"Quién va? Quién es?" called Paco, echoing the same challenge in Spanish.

"Halt or I'll shoot," came the order again.

"Wait, Paco!" cried Peter. "Think of Limik!"

It was a timely reminder. Paco was on the verge of spurring the mule and riding down the voice from the shadows.

"Get down and lead your animals," came the command. "Walk on up to the house there, nice and easy-like."

The metal triangle hanging on the porch for calling the vaqueros to meals began an insistent ringing. The sounds of the shouted confrontation on the road had reached the soldiers in the Reed home. There was a muffled stir of cursing and swearing, the thump of boots running out onto the hardwood porch mixing with the flap of bare feet.

"That's far enough," called the sentry from behind Peter and Paco.

On the porch, Peter could see a disheveled array of soldiers in various stages of undress. Some stood with

uniform blouses hanging out, and others wore suspenders over bare chests.

In the center of the group posed a little man with
round shoulders. A rumpled ring of hair stood straight
out all around his crown as if he had slept standing on
his head. He held a pistol in front of his bulging pot
belly.

"What is this, Hollis? What have we got here?" demanded the little man.

"Well, sir, Lieutenant Falls, sir, I caught these two
sneakin' up on the house."

"We were not sneaking!" Peter corrected. "This is
my home. What are *you* doing here? And where is my
mother?"

"Ah, the coyote pup!" said Falls, snorting. "I'll ask
the questions here, sonny boy, unless you want the same
treatment your father got!"

The Americanos of Commodore Stockton had stolen
every ham from the smokehouse of Will Reed before
they sailed away. The commodore himself had tasted a
fresh-cooked slice of the stuff and declared that Señor
Reed's mind might be addled from living among the
Mexicans, but that only a truehearted American knew
how to smoke a ham so well.

Lieutenant Falls, however, had a different impres-
sion of the Reed family. He envisioned a different purpose for the empty smokehouse; adobe walls and slit
windows made it a perfect jail.

Francesca faced off with the pompous little man
who held his pistol tight at the back of Peter's neck.

"This is madness!" she declared. "You cannot take

my son prisoner in his own home!"

"He has broken the regulations, madam, and he is my prisoner!"

Conscious of the cold steel against his flesh, Peter did not speak or move. He kept his gaze riveted on his mother, whose eyes burned with fury and indignation at the injustice.

"But he did not know your rules! How *could* he know them? He has only just returned home!"

Oblivious to her protest, Falls licked his buck teeth in thought and then began to recite his orders. "It is plain as anything. He broke the rules. Out after ten o'clock. Carrying a weapon. Traveling with a companion. Strictly against the rules."

Baby Limik, being nursed by the cook, gave a contented cry from the parlor. Francesca gestured toward the sound.

"Traveling with this child, señor! Bringing this baby home so that it might be cared for! He has told you how he and Paco came to be on the road so late! Are you a man without reason?"

Again, Falls ticked off the broken rules. "On the road after ten o'clock. Traveling with a companion. Carrying a weapon . . . I can name another dozen regulations broken if you like, madam. Enough to get this boy of yours strung up. Neither Commodore Stockton nor any other American will doubt my reason in this. Your son is plainly a menace. A danger to me and my men here!" His eyes flared as he said these words, and Francesca could see that he actually believed what he was telling her. She stood face-to-face with a madman who hid his insanity behind rules and regulations and imagined threats.

Peter also understood. He looked at her with an expression like Will's, telling her that she must tread gently. Here was a coiled snake, prepared to strike. Like a rattler, Lieutenant Falls perceived any step too near as a danger and a challenge to his petty tyranny. And there could be no doubt that he would kill without provocation if he believed he was being threatened.

"I insist that my son's case be heard by Commodore Stockton! You are the commandante, but the commodore is the governor." She played to his self-importance now, submitting to his imagined authority while appealing to a higher authority to decide the issue.

The ploy seemed to placate Falls. He stepped back a pace from Peter, removing the muzzle of the weapon from his neck. "Now you see, madam. I am only doing my job. Rules are rules. I obey authority, and so must you. If the rules are broken, it is my job to enforce them. It is for Commodore Stockton to interpret the fate of your son, whether he is hanged or imprisoned. Rules are rules, you see. My duty . . ."

Francesca had seen enough to know that Falls, when pushed, was quite capable of executing his own interpretation and judgment of the rules. A chill of fear coursed through her.

"If Peter gives his word of honor that he will not run away, may he not remain your prisoner in this house?"

To this, Falls shook his head. "I already explained to you, madam, that prisoners would be confined to the smokehouse. He's lucky I do not simply hang him and this Indian from that oak tree and be done with the bother. Commodore Stockton would not question me if I did. They broke the rules. No matter whose son he might be. No matter. Men have been known to use the cover of carrying a child as hostage to protect themselves when they intend to do harm to the authorities." This was a new possibility. An interpretation which he enjoyed contemplating. Perhaps that was the real reason Peter had been traveling with the baby.

Francesca saw the madness flash through his eyes again. How might she stop it from taking root? She stepped closer to Peter, taking him by the arm as though he were a child caught in a prank.

"Well then, Peter, you shall have to stay in the smokehouse. The Commandante Falls must obey authority no matter what the circumstances, even though the rules were violated in innocence. But he is not an inhumane man—simply an officer forced to do some distasteful things. He will allow me to feed you and Paco, and bring you bedding. You must go along to the smokehouse. You and Paco. It is the law, and we must obey as Commandante Falls obeys."

Placated by her soft voice and seeming compliance, Falls flashed his buck teeth in a proud smile. He squared his sloping shoulders and nodded his head to her in what he imagined was a chivalrous manner. "Well now, madam, I see that you have some sense. You understand I am just doing my job."

"I would like to walk beside my son to the jail." Francesca took Peter's arm. "I have not seen him in a while and would like his company if only for these few moments. A mother's wish, Commandante Falls." She said this so sweetly that he did not deny her. Even so, he still held the pistol aimed squarely at the back of Peter's head as they marched out to the smokehouse.

———

The little bay horse Will had purchased near Yerba Buena for Fowler to ride could not keep up with Flotada. The ranchero, now dressed in his buckskins, chafed at the delay. The farther south they rode, the more it sounded as though the war would soon be on the front doorstep of his home, if it was not already.

With Yerba Buena and Monterey both controlled by the Bear Flaggers, return to Santa Barbara by ship was out of the question. Will's splinted arm was bound tightly to his chest, but it was his own impatience that caused him the greatest irritation.

Once again it was necessary to rein in Flotada, whose easy canter ate up the miles, to allow the winded bay to catch his breath. "Fowler," Will said, "either I need to go on alone or we need to get you better mounted."

Tor Fowler slowed the laboring brown horse to a walk and felt the animal's sides heaving. "We can't afford to get parted," he said firmly. "You'd be in trouble with an American outfit or with them Mexes that held me prisoner, either one. Besides, I can't go back till we meet up with Fremont and explain . . . I'm a deserter, see?"

"All right then, it's a change of mounts that's needed. We'll see what we can find."

They rode along the Salinas River, south of Monterey. The course of the stream bed would eventually lead them into the heart of what the old Spaniards had named the *Temblor*, the earthquake range. But the part through which they rode was a wide, dusty valley, dotted with oak trees, small ranches, and occasional grizzly bears.

A wisp of smoke from one of the branch arroyos

drew Will's attention. "Let's see if we can do some quick trading," he called to Tor, and turned aside into the canyon.

A hot breeze swirled the smell of smoke down to the riders. There was something else on the wind besides smoke, something that made Flotada snort and stiffen his knees in his trot as though protesting their course.

The ranchero sensed the tension in the spirited horse and caught the need for caution in approaching the ranch. Fowler carried Will's Hawken rifle, while Will clenched a pistol in his left hand along with the reins.

The dwelling was on a bench of land above the canyon. Motioning for Will to halt his horse at the near approach, Tor rode past on the trail till he flanked the home at another gully.

Will heard the perfectly imitated plaintive song of a dove: low note, middle note, three sustained low notes. So realistic was the call that Will waited for the sound to be repeated just to be certain it was really the signal.

Then, putting the spurs to Flotada, Will urged the gray into instant movement. Up the trail they sprinted, then turned aside to climb a bank at the last second so as to appear from an unexpected direction.

The ranch house was a smoldering ruin. The roof had been burned, and its collapse had pulled down two of the adobe walls. In the dirt of the cleared space before the door lay a dead man. Flies buzzed around his face and swarmed thickly on the dark blood that pooled under his chest. In his hands he clutched no weapons, only beef jerky and a stack of tortillas. The shattered remains of a clay water jug were scattered around.

"He was bringing them something to eat when they shot him down," Fowler said angrily. The mountain man stepped down off the bay, which he tied to a corral post. The gate had been yanked free of the fence and the tracks of five or six stampeded horses showed in the dust. "Run off all the stock, too," Tor concluded.

Examining the dead man while Fowler went into what remained of the house, Will called, "This man's been dead only since yesterday. They may be only hours ahead of us."

Fowler stepped back out of the ruined adobe and circled around the narrow bench of land, checking behind the corral fence.

Will saw him stop beside a row of trees, then turn away suddenly and lean on the rail as if sick. "There's a woman here," Fowler called. "They . . . she . . . she's dead too."

———

Two mounds of earth stretched side by side beneath the shade of a nearby live oak. "Best we can do for now," Will said, putting the shovel in the ground at the head of one grave. "We still need to find you a better horse. We'll get somebody to fetch the priest to tell their kin."

"I bet the devils who did this are running off all the stock," Fowler observed. "From their tracks I'd say a dozen men were here. They could be raiding all the ranchos hereabouts and driving a herd along with them."

Will saw Flotada's ears prick forward, and the horse gazed pointedly toward a willow grove below the hillside. Indicating for Fowler to be silent, Will stepped next to the trunk of the oak. Laying the pistol across his splinted arm, he drew a bead on the center of the grove.

When he glanced back toward Fowler, Will saw that the mountain man was already ghosting from tree to tree down the slope. In the patches of light and shadow thrown down by the willows and the oaks, Fowler's tawny buckskin form was zig-zagging, lionlike, from cover to cover.

Fowler was no more than halfway down the slope when Will heard a rustling in the willows, followed by the nicker of a horse. Both men froze, guns at the ready, then a riderless buckskin horse limped out of the brush.

It was a tall lineback buckskin with a dark mane and four black legs. Fowler and Will still watched the willows intently until certain this was no trick. At last the flinty-faced scout approached the gelding and slipped a rawhide string around his neck. The horse stood patiently waiting, favoring a foreleg and holding his weight up off it.

"This'd be one the cutthroats rode in here," Fowler remarked, pointing to the outline left by a sweat-soaked saddle blanket. "Left him 'cause he's lamed."

Will inspected the horse's brand as Fowler ran his hands gingerly down the injured leg. "I know this brand," Will remarked. "This is one of Mariano Vallejo's prize animals, from his ranch near Sonoma."

"Well, lookee here," Fowler said, picking up the hoof and digging into the sole with his sheath knife. A jagged shard of clay pot fell out into his hand. "Probably came from the busted water jug when they killed that feller. Reckon he'll be sound again now."

The horse planted his forefoot firmly on the ground to indicate that Fowler's conclusion was correct. "Get your stuff and get mounted," Will said. "You won't have any trouble keeping up now."

CHAPTER 13

The herd of horses being driven along left a trail as plain to the two experienced trackers as a well-marked roadway. The tracks headed south, keeping to the washes and gullies, out of sight of the main road and following the line of hills.

At one point the trail forked, with the milling mass of horses being diverted into low-lying pasture near a spring. The tracks of three horses with riders, noticeable because they stayed three abreast and did not cross one another's paths, continued on. "I 'spect they left the others hereabouts with the stolen stock while them three reconnoitered up yonder," commented Fowler, waving his arms toward a hill that loomed just ahead.

"It could be worse than that," Will observed. "Seems somebody in that group knows this country like I do. There's another rancho just over that rise."

The American scout and the California rancher exchanged looks. Each saw mirrored in the other's strong features his own grim thoughts: *What would they find across the hill?*

The two men checked their weapons and separated at the base of the hill to again make their approaches from opposite directions. Will's route led to a low-lying saddle. There was very little cover once Flotada had climbed out of the cottonwoods and mesquite along the creek bottom—almost a bare hillside with a few clumps of brush and granite boulders. Will dismounted, tied the gray horse to a tree branch and crept up the hillside. If his memory served, the ranch was just on the other side.

Tor Fowler saw all this from his vantage point high on the hillside to the west. He and the buckskin had climbed almost straight up the slope before moving toward the ridgeline that lay between him and the ranch. Fowler watched Will's cautious progress up the bare hill of dry grass and foxtails. Automatically his eyes traced Will's probable path from boulder to boulder until it topped the rise.

There, just at the summit of the hill, in a small cluster of rocks, a flash of light caught his eye. It could have been sun glinting off a patch of quartz or an outcropping of mica, but as the scout watched, the flash was repeated. This time he could detect movement as well. Fowler was certain he was looking at the reflection off a gun barrel.

The watcher was obviously posted to guard the hillside up which Will was sneaking. Even if he had not seen Will Reed yet, there was no way the ranchero could cross the largest bare space near the ridgeline without being spotted and shot.

Fowler could fire a warning shot of his own that would alert his friend, but if the other murderers were nearby it would bring them all into the action. "Ain't no kinda choice," he muttered to the buckskin. "Come on then, hoss," he said. "Let's go down there to help him."

As fast and as noiselessly as possible, Fowler and the buckskin plunged down the slope. As they went, Tor was grateful that the sun was westering. Its descent toward the hills behind him would make him harder to spot if the guard should glance his way.

The next time Fowler had a clear view of the ridgeline, he had dropped too low to see Will. But the scout could guess his friend's whereabouts: The watcher in the circle of rocks was standing now, swinging his rifle from point to point as he covered Will's approach, holding his fire till he was certain of killing range.

A woodpecker hammered on a hollow tree nearby, marking the passing like the ticking of a fast-running clock. Fowler knew that the explosion of a rifle would soon be the chime that ended the hour, perhaps marking the death of Will Reed as well.

Flicking the reins against the buckskin's rear with a loud pop, horse and rider exploded downhill toward the waiting assassin. Fowler began screaming at the top of his lungs to distract the watcher, who stood to draw a bead on the unsuspecting Will.

The figure in the rocks whirled around, startled by the spectacle—a tall apparition whose leather clothing blended with the animal he rode until both appeared as one. The charging beast thundered down the hill, as unstoppable as an avalanche and just as deadly.

Firing one futile shot that came nowhere near Fowler, the guard made no attempt to reload. He threw down his rifle and fled. Tor was behind him at once, the buckskin's pounding hooves right at his heels.

The man was brought up against a rock, his sombrero gone and one sandal missing. "Don't even twitch," Fowler ordered, leveling the rifle across the saddle horn, "unless you figure having a big hole in your chest would make for interestin' conversation."

"No hablo inglés, señor," the man said, holding his empty hands aloft.

Fowler noted the ragged cutoff homespun trousers and the single remaining hemp sandal. "Hey, Reed," Fowler yelled, "come up here pronto!"

Will soon appeared atop the ridge. "Somehow I don't figure this feller for one of them horse-thievin' murderers," Fowler said.

A few moments of conversation explained the true situation. The paisano, whose name was Feliz, was guarding against the *return* of the horse thieves. They had raided the rancho only the day before. "My brother, he is shot at the door of our casa, but he manages to wound one of the ladrones, the robbers. They do not see me and they ride away when we start shooting. We think perhaps they will circle back and try again, and so, I watch."

Will asked if they could have food and water. He explained about what they had found at the neighboring rancho.

Feliz gasped; then his face hardened. "My brother is only a little wounded," he said. "He can stay to guard our rancho, and I will ride with you. We will hang those malditos, or shoot them down like wild dogs. Give me but an hour, and six will ride with you."

———

News of Padilla's bandits reached the Reed Rancho when a half-starved young vaquero stumbled out of the mountains in search of refuge. Instead, he was captured by Falls, refused food or water, and forced to march at gunpoint to the rancho.

He collapsed on the steps of the servants' quarters as Falls glared down at him. "He pretends not to understand English." Falls did not step down from his horse as Francesca and Simona rushed to aid the half-conscious vaquero.

"Agua," begged the prisoner, who was no older than Peter.

"Hey there!" Falls commanded as Simona brought the drinking gourd. "He can have water after he explains who he is and where he comes from."

Francesca glared at Falls and took the gourd from Simona. Never taking her eyes from the little tyrant, she held the water to the lips of the vaquero, who drank eagerly.

"It is not wise to defy me, madam," warned Falls.

"He will not be able to tell you anything unless he drinks."

Falls stepped from his horse, took two steps, and kicked the gourd from the man's hands. "If he wants any more he will tell me what I want to know."

Holding the young man's head, Francesca spoke to him softly, carefully explaining the presence of Falls. The vaquero licked his parched lips and lay his head in Francesca's arms.

"The Americanos here," he croaked. "And the bandits of Padilla just to the north. Both . . . they take what they wish. Rape our mothers and sisters and kill . . . everyone . . . except I alone escaped." He closed his eyes. His chin trembled with emotion as the vision of horror replayed in his mind. "*Por el bien del país* . . . Padilla claims he kills for the good of the country. Just as this one." He opened his eyes to glare at Falls. "This *diablo huero*, the white devil who denies me water."

"Is Padilla coming this way?" Francesca asked as Falls leaned closer, trying to comprehend if their conversation contained some treachery.

"He goes where he wishes." The vaquero closed his eyes again as though he had no strength to hold them open.

Francesca instructed Simona to prepare food and draw water to soak the vaquero's bloody feet.

Falls stomped onto the porch. "You must tell me in English what you are saying! What is this Mexican spy telling you, madam? I demand to know the truth!"

"He is the only survivor of an attack by a bandit troop headed by a villain named Padilla." She answered honestly, but Falls had already made up his mind. He had written his own tale of how the half-dead young man came to the Reed Rancho.

"Lies, I am certain. It is obvious . . . he is a survivor, all right, but no doubt he has survived a battle against our American forces! Look at him! Mexican! You cannot expect me to be such a fool as to believe that there is some rogue Mexican bandit on the rampage in the north, killing his own people?" He snorted his derision at such a thought.

"Think whatever you wish, el cabro!" Francesca snapped, smoothing back the vaquero's matted hair. "Look at him! He is in no condition to lie!"

"Unless he has been on the run from our American forces and now finds himself my prisoner. Reason enough for a Mexican to invent such a tale!" He called to the guards at the smokehouse. "We have another prisoner! On the double!"

Francesca leaned over the vaquero protectively. "He is injured! He needs food and care or he may die! I cannot allow you to do this! We will care for him here!"

Falls placed his boot on the arm of the limp vaquero. "You cannot allow me, madam?" He sneered at her defiance. "You question my authority?"

"I question your humanity!" Francesca spat. "And your sanity in such a case!"

Simona emerged with a plate of corn bread and a bowl of cold soup. Falls struck the tray from the hands of the startled cook.

"I did not give permission for him to be fed. Unless he tells the truth, he shall not be fed, madam! That is the final word."

"And if he has told you all there is to tell?"

"Bandits? Absurd! He has met this fate at the hands of my countrymen. He is fleeing justice and thinks I am stupid enough to believe that he should be allowed to stay in a house and be fed and nursed to strength so he can kill us when our backs are turned! I am no fool, madam."

"He must be fed."

"In our little jail, perhaps. When he confesses, perhaps. When I give my permission. Then . . . perhaps, madam, he will be fed. Now stand back from him or you shall find I can be a harsh man . . . even with stiff-necked women." He clenched his fists as though he would strike her.

Simona pulled at her shoulder. "Por favor, señora Reed!" she cried.

Francesca lowered her eyes and moved away from

the unconscious vaquero. He was half dragged, half carried to the smokehouse and thrown in like a sack of potatoes. Then the door was slammed shut and locked again.

CHAPTER 14

The rounded slopes, covered with dense chaparral, trailed streamers of wet, gray fog. "I smell the ocean in this mist," Fowler said. "Is it that near?"

Gesturing toward the west, Will Reed indicated the line of hills that rose above the saddle they were crossing. "No more than fifteen, maybe twenty miles that direction. Reminds me of home."

What he did not say was that home was always uppermost in his thoughts, and had been for the endless miles of riding. Will wished he could see across the intervening space, see Francesca and know that she was safe and their home untouched by either the lunatic Falls or the evil-hearted Padilla. Will comforted himself more than once on the foresight of having sent Peter out of harm's way.

Behind the two Americans rode a score of vaqueros and rancheros gathered from the valley as the men rode south. All agreed that the safety of their families was more important than the politics of nations or the nationality of the perpetrators. They were bound together by their honor to rid the countryside of malditos and ladrones, evil men and thieves. *Por el bien del país* . . . for the good of the country.

Will shook himself out of his reverie. "Down below

this pass is the little mission town of San Luis Obispo. We'll get food and rest the horses there, then press on south. With hard riding and God's help we can make Santa Barbara by tomorrow."

Down the slope they rode until the mission itself came into view. The church sat on a knob that stood out in the surrounding bowl of green hillsides and jagged rocky outcroppings. One wing of the building, two stories high, stood at right angles to a low colonnaded portico. The mission and the church looked peaceful; a decided contrast to the uneasiness in Will's heart.

With only a mile of green pastures edged in yellow bee plant and mustard weed yet to cross, a line of riders emerged from the cottonwoods bordering the small creek below the mission. The mounted men obviously intended to challenge the progress of Will's group; the newcomers spread out in a line directly across the ranchero's path. Will called a halt and both sides studied the other intently.

After a long moment Fowler announced, "It ain't Padilla. Them's buckskins on that tall fella, and the others ain't dressed Mexican neither. Yup, they's Americans."

There was a hasty conference with Will's band. "What will you do, Don Reed?" he was asked. "They are your countrymen."

Will shook his head. "California is my country. We did not come to fight the war to decide which nation will rule," he said. "We will not fight these men if they will let us pass. But if they will not—" He shrugged. "Then see to my family after."

Holding aloft a saddle blanket in token of parley, Tor Fowler and Will rode across the field toward the waiting line of men. As they drew closer Fowler glanced at Will's sling-bound arm and commented, "Get ready to make a run for it. I recognize that tall, skinny fella. That's Andrew Jackson Sinnickson, one of the Bear Flag leaders."

"That's close enough, Fowler," ordered the swarthy-complected Sinnickson when the men were still twenty yards apart. "I never figured you for a traitor."

"Sinnickson," Fowler replied, "me and Will Reed here got a story to tell you. You have the reputation of being a fair man. What say you listen first and make up your mind after?"

Fifteen minutes later Sinnickson asked, "God's truth then, Fowler? Davis lied about who started the fighting, and Falls murdered two youngsters in cold blood, but right now you're trailing a gang of cutthroat Mexicans?"

Will answered for them both. "That's it," he said simply. "There's wickedness on both sides, and it looks like Santa Barbara and my family are about to be caught in the middle. Will you let us pass?"

Pondering for a minute, Sinnickson dropped his head in thought, like a great carrion bird perched on a limb. At last he said, "Pass, nothing. It's time the grizzly banner stood for what's right. We'll ride with you."

After an hour of rest and some food, the group of riders who had followed Will Reed and Tor Fowler from the north were ready to move on southward. But when they rode out of the grassy bottom land dedicated to Saint Louis the Bishop, their numbers had swollen by twenty more.

Behind the leading rank of mountain men in tawny buckskin rode the oddest collection of fighters California had ever seen. Elegantly dressed rancheros astride impatient stallions were flanked by frontiersmen in loose coats of leather tied with rawhide strings. The untrimmed hair of the rough trappers escaped their drooping hats, and their wiry beards were a sharp contrast to the rancheros' smooth faces. Raggedly clothed *paisanos*, the simple farmers and ranchers of California, rode their short, stocky horses next to stony-faced Indian scouts.

If the California Republic was to have any meaning, Sinnickson had explained to the group, all men who desired to live peaceably had to be able to receive justice and oppose evil, wherever it was found. Will was grateful for the strength of men at his back, but as they rode out, his thoughts all lay on what he would find ahead.

Simona nursed baby Limik as Francesca prepared the evening meal for prisoners and guards as well.

"Every day you fix supper for these Americano pigs," Simona said indignantly. "Let me prepare it, señora Reed, and I shall add a drop or two of something special to their beans. Then we shall see how well they are able to guard the smokehouse!"

"You think I have not been tempted to do as much?" Francesca sighed as she dished up the corn bread. "Then I imagined what that devil Falls would do if he suspected we poisoned their food. No, Simona. We must try to outsmart *señor Diablo Huero*, Lord White Devil, until Will returns. He would want us to stay calm and outthink this fellow until my good husband can put things right. Then I believe this Lieutenant Falls will find himself in grave trouble with the Americano leaders. If we can last . . ." Her brow furrowed. "I must hold my tongue with this beast."

"He is *muy peligroso,* very dangerous, señora Reed. I am frightened to think what he might do."

Francesca nodded and tucked Will's Bible into the pocket of her apron. The condition of the young vaquero had worsened since yesterday, and Peter said he begged for a priest. Falls had forbidden a priest to be summoned, but surely Peter could comfort the young man by reading from the Holy Scriptures. She had bribed the guard by making a fine berry cobbler. Falls had ridden into Santa Barbara. Could they object to her giving the Bible to Peter?

"Who goes there?" The youngest of the two marine guards challenged her as she approached.

"I have brought your supper," Francesca answered sweetly.

"I smelled that corn bread coming before you got halfway here," called the second guard cheerfully. They were pleasant enough with Francesca, but she knew they were much like dogs, wagging happily until the moment their master ordered them to attack.

"Simona and I made a cobbler for you today." She offered them the heaping plates, then waited silently as they unlocked the door of the smokehouse.

"You'll have to show us your pockets, ma'am. Them's the rules, and Lieutenant Falls will have our heads if we don't follow them."

She pulled the pockets of her apron out for them to examine and produced the well-worn Bible. "My son has asked for his father's Bible to read in these long days of his confinement. Surely you cannot object."

They thumbed through it, exchanged glances and shrugged. "It ain't like it's a weapon, now, is it?" Stepping aside, they let her pass into the gloomy interior of the cell.

The sweet scent of woodsmoke and ham greeted her. Peter and Paco were against the far wall. The young vaquero, who was called José, lay on a blanket in the center of the enclosure. In spite of the thick adobe walls, the air was close and too warm. The light from the guards' lantern shone on the haggard faces of the prisoners. Francesca was forbidden to speak in Spanish. Violation of this order would be reported in spite of berry cobbler bribes, and Falls would punish the prisoners by withholding their food.

"Two minutes, Missus Reed," called the guard.

Two minutes. Just long enough to kneel and check José's weak pulse.

"Has he eaten since yesterday?" Francesca asked Peter.

"Only a bite. I think . . . he wants to die, Mother. This Padilla is very bad. José tells us that his sisters and mother were . . . murdered. And I think he has given up all hope."

Francesca gave Peter the Bible. "You must find hope here. Read to him. This is our only comfort, Peter. Your father would say the same if he were here. This is our best weapon."

Peter held the Bible to the light. He nodded and then embraced the book. "All men seem evil to me now, Mother. All . . . the Americanos of my father's homeland. Men like Padilla, who are from this, my own country. Who is for us, Mother? And who is for the innocent ones . . . like baby Limik? These days the darkness seems to consume everything."

"It has always been the same, Peter." She touched his forehead as though she were tucking him in. "There have always been men like Lieutenant Falls who make themselves grand by bullying others. And there have always been those like Padilla . . . and the British who brought plagues upon a gentle people without a thought or care that their whole world has vanished now." She passed the plate to Paco. "God's Word is filled with such stories. Injustice. Evil. But I tell you this, Peter, the Lord is still God and these men will stand before Him as judge. Sometimes that is the only hope we have left to cling to in this world."

"Thirty seconds, Missus Reed," came the warning.

"Es la hora de rezar," she whispered. "It is time for prayer, Peter!"

"What was that you're saying Missus Reed? You speaking Mexican, are you?" The lantern behind her was raised higher.

"Just reminding my son to say his prayers," she replied with a strained cheerfulness. She kissed Peter on his forehead. "Pray, Peter. Pray that the Lord will deliver us from evil just like you carried the baby home to our care."

The boy nodded. "Yes, Mother, I will."

"Time! Out you go, Missus Reed. Visiting is over!"

CHAPTER 15

Two of Mitchell's sailors and a pair of Falls' marines were deeply involved in their game of horseshoes. The score was three games to two in favor of the marines when the clatter of hooves and swirling dust alerted them to the approach of horses.

All reached for their rifles in alarm at the racket, but it was difficult to feel very apprehensive. After all, Santa Barbara had been peaceful under Falls' restrictive rules. If the Barbareños were not happy, at least they had not shown open hostility. Still, it was best to be on guard, so no one relaxed until the new arrivals appeared as a herd of horses only, rather than a troop of mounted men.

The American sailor on guard duty on the outskirts of the parade ground next to the old presidio gave the order to halt, but in the mass of milling animals it was unclear where there were humans to hear the command. "Halt!" he ordered again when a rider at last came into view.

Four Fingers looked disgusted with the blue jacket's tone. "Qué dice la vaca? What does the cow say?" he muttered. His right hand crept downward to the reata, and he shook out a loop on the side of the horse where the guard could not see.

The sentry, who spoke no Spanish, knew only that the rider gave no sign of complying and was openly carrying a knife. Its handle could be seen protruding above the sash around the waist of Four Fingers. The sailor raised the still uncocked weapon to his shoulder and repeated the order to halt.

The hand that gave Four Fingers his name flashed across the neck of his sorrel horse. The loop hit the guard in the face with such force that he wondered if one of his friends had thrown a horseshoe at him.

In the next second the loop flipped around his shoulders, pinning his arms to his sides. Before his rifle even hit the ground, the sailor was jerked off his feet and dragged across the parade ground.

"Ha!" shouted Padilla with delight, waving his sombrero over his shoulder. "Bring them on, amigos," he yelled to the other riders. "Stampede!"

The herd of thirty stomping, kicking horses veered sharply onto the parade ground, scattering the sailors and marines. Two shots were fired, but neither hit anything.

Padilla drove his strawberry roan directly at a fleeing marine. "Golpe de caballo!" Padilla exulted as the horse's shoulder struck the American in the back and knocked him down on his face. "Golpe de caballo!" he called to his comrades. "Strike with the horse!"

Four Fingers spurred his mount toward the abandoned fort. The Americans were fleeing in that direction, and Four Fingers wanted to deny them the shelter of the crumbling adobe walls. The pace of the red horse was slowed by his kicking and crow-hopping at the weight of the still-struggling man being dragged behind. Four Fingers never slackened his gallop, but with a nonchalant air, he loosened the dally around the horn and let the reata slip to the ground. Two of the stampeding horses jumped the torn and bruised figure without touching him, and he hugged the earth and remained flat on his belly.

The slight delay had given two of the Americans the chance to reach the cover of the presidio. The pair still had their rifles and, once out of the immediate terror of the stampede, they began a deliberate and methodical process of firing and reloading.

The battle of the parade ground was over just that suddenly. Padilla wheeled the roan toward the edge of the field as soon as the firing started. He waved the Colt revolving rifle, and the others joined him there, out of the effective range of the Americans' weapons.

Gesturing for Four Fingers to ride to his side, Padilla said to the other banditos, "Keep the herd here, amigos, and watch that the Americanos do not break out. We will find out the strength of the Yankee dogs in the pueblo and return here for you."

As he and Four Fingers set off on the short ride into town, Padilla complimented his second-in-command. "That was a marvelous cast you made, amigo. Truly you are a lazadore bravo!"

Four Fingers made a deprecating gesture. "Not so good, Capitan. I did not hit what I was aiming for."

"You caught the gringo completely around his body," argued Padilla. "What more would you have?"

"Ah," sighed Four Fingers, "I was trying for his neck!"

———

The afternoon heat was stifling as Francesca carried

the midday meal to the smokehouse jail.

The chains on Peter's ankles had been forged by the Santa Barbara blacksmith only yesterday. Francesca blinked back tears of fury as the door of the smokehouse slammed shut, leaving her son and Paco in utter darkness.

"I will come back with supper for you," she said in Spanish, breaking the English-only rule of Falls.

"And a lamp, Mother." Peter's voice sounded small, yet unafraid.

Falls nudged her hard away from the slit window. "You are to speak only in English, madam!" Falls growled. "I have spoken to you about that before. This prisoner is already under suspicion. How do I know if he is passing you some information? Perhaps some word from the enemy."

Francesca whirled around to face him, her patience finally at an end. "And who is the enemy, el cabro? Qué grosero! How insolent you are to speak of enemies when you sleep in the bed of my son and he is chained to the walls of his father's smokehouse! You steal our food and then lock my son into this place as though he were nothing more than meat! I ask you again, el cabro, Who is the enemy in this country? It is not Peter. Nor Paco. Nor myself. It is not we who have stolen and persecuted and even forbidden the gathering to worship God!"

Her outburst startled the little man. He had not expected such a reaction. "What I do I do for the sake of my duty. For the good of the country." He drew himself up. "You are ungrateful, madam. I could have this upstart hanged for a spy. No one would question my decision. I have executed others no older than he for the good of the country and no one questioned—"

"Por el bien del país!" she scoffed.

"English, madam!"

"For the good of the country, you say? I have heard this lie before. You know nothing of this country or of our ways. You have seen our land and desired to take it."

"And we shall have it, madam. No matter if you wish it not to happen. You and that traitorous husband of yours, who is also rotting in jail in the north!" He enjoyed watching the blow of this information.

Silenced, Francesca suddenly felt sick. "What do you know of my husband?"

He chuckled—a low, mocking laugh. Her pain was his amusement for the day. "He went to investigate the execution of two young spies, did he not? Two spies no older than your son, madam. Executed for the good of the country."

"Ramon and Carlos . . ." She faltered, looking at a man whose soul was the blackest she had ever known in a human. "It was you . . . you killed them."

He shrugged, unconcerned. "The country is full of spies . . . and former Americans. Traitors. Like your husband, madam. Perhaps like your own son?"

The threat was clear. What he had done to others he would do again. Perhaps he had also murdered Will. "Why are you here?"

"I thought my purpose was obvious, madam." He gestured toward the door of the smokehouse. "To hang the dead meat over a slow fire before it spoils and stinks up the land. I, madam, am a patriot. Here for my country. We will have no opposition left when the task is complete."

"*Usted es un diablero lunático!* You are a demon lunatic!"

"Perhaps, madam. But I am efficient, am I not?" Her accusation amused him. He was not surprised at her outburst any longer. She was a wife and a mother, after all. No doubt she knew the twins he had shot down in the north. And she was not an American. She could not understand that this land must be joined to the United States at all costs.

"I do not believe all Americanos are so cruel as you. You do not do this for the sake of the land. You kill and bully because it gives you great pleasure to do so. The rest is only an excuse. Fear God, you demon. His judgment is true."

To this he laughed. "So. It is as I suspected, madam. You are a little hypocrite yourself. You have opposed me all along." He stepped near, and she could smell his foul breath. "Well, now, that puts a different light on the relationship. Does it not? No more pretending, madam." He grabbed her arm. "Now we can maybe get to know each other a little better. On honest terms. Come along with me."

She cried out as he pulled her toward the bushes. In the smokehouse Peter shouted for him to stop, to leave Francesca alone!

Francesca lashed out at Falls, kicking him hard in the leg. She dug her nails into his arm and struck his face as he tried to kiss her.

"You think I care?" He enjoyed her struggle, slapping her hard across the cheek and jerking her hair until she screamed from the pain.

Helpless in his prison, Peter slammed his fists against the adobe walls. The ring of his chains echoed like the thrashing of an animal caught in a steel trap.

"Let her go! In the name of God! Let my mother go!"

Again she struck at Falls, this time drawing blood. He twisted her wrist, bringing her to her knees. Touching his cheek, he looked at his own blood and then wiped it on her face as she wept.

"Do not do this to me!" she begged. "Do not dishonor me!"

"Hear how she whines." He showed his teeth. "I have not enjoyed such sport in a long time, madam. Yes! Fight me! Fight me, then! You will not be laughing behind your hand when I am finished with you!" He gave another hard twist of her wrist and hooked his fingers in the lace collar of her dress. "I enjoy an honest fight, mada—"

Falls did not see the determined figure behind him. The large iron skillet in Simona's hand came down on his head and rang like the sound of a gong when it connected.

The eyes of *el cabro* rolled back in his head. He swayed above Francesca for an instant and then collapsed in a heap on the ground.

Simona gave his head another solid blow with the skillet for good measure. She towered over him as Francesca scrambled away, standing far back from his motionless form.

"Un mulo muy malo!" Simona declared. "A very evil mule, this animal!" She flourished the skillet and turned to her mistress. "He will learn not to turn his back on a woman with a skillet!" At the sight of Francesca's swollen cheek, her confident demeanor vanished. "Oh, Doña Reed!" she cried. "If only we had not buried the guns, I would shoot this devil myself!"

Francesca embraced Simona. "You have done well. This fool did not imagine to banish frying pans from

Santa Barbara! You have tailed the steer, Simona! Now we must get the keys and release Peter and Paco, then decide what we must do before the other Americanos come back!"

———

The bells of the mission clanged wildly as Francesca and Simona struggled to free the prisoners from the smokehouse. "I will keep trying, Simona," Francesca said. "You go see what this alarm is about."

Up the lane ran a ragged band of marines. There were only a handful of them, and half had no weapons. "Lieutenant! Lieutenant! The Mexicans have busted loose in a rampage down to the—where's Lieutenant Falls?" Hollis demanded of Simona.

"Cómo?" she said, all innocence. "No hablo, señor."

"Blast it all, woman! Uh, donda esta Lieutenant Falls? Falls . . . you know, el cabro?"

"Ah, sí, el cabro," Simona nodded. With her frying pan she gestured back down the hill toward town.

"You mean he ain't here?"

From around the side of the hacienda nearest the smokehouse came the sound of a hammer pounding against links of chain. "What's goin' on in there?" Hollis wondered aloud. "Come on," he said to the six other panting soldiers, "let's check around here real quick. Somethin' ain't right."

They rushed toward the smokehouse, with Simona loudly protesting in Spanish that el cabro had left. The smokehouse cell was open, and Francesca was hammering at the chains that bound Peter's legs.

"Hold it right there," demanded Hollis, leveling his

carbine at the group. "What have you done with the lieutenant?"

From the oleander bushes came a slurred reply. "I'm right here."

Out of the brush staggered Falls, holding one hand against the back of his head and swearing loudly when he stepped into the bright sunlight. Two lines of blood had trickled from his scalp around to the corners of his mouth, painting him with a grotesque smile like a monstrous clown. "These lousy Mexicans tried to kill me," he said. "We're gonna shoot 'em all, right now. Line 'em up against the wall." He gestured with his gore-covered right hand toward the smokehouse.

"Lieutenant," said the young marine nervously. "Sir, we was just run out of Santa Barbara by a gang of armed Mexicans. Mitchell's holed up down at the mission, but the rest of us couldn't make that, so we hightailed it up here. We think they'll be comin' after us too."

Falls glanced around at the rancho. "Too few of us to defend this place," he said. "We'll retreat up into the hills. Make 'em pay to get at us."

"What about these prisoners, sir?"

"Lock 'em up again," Falls said, "all except this one." He grasped Francesca roughly by the arm with his bloody hand. "She's coming with us."

———

Padilla and his men arrived at the Reed Rancho with a pack of horses and mules piled high with plunder. From the top of one hastily wrapped canvas protruded a golden candlestick.

"Ah," said Four Fingers in an admiring tone as he

looked up at the Reed home. "I will enjoy getting acquainted with this house."

"Later," Padilla snapped. "First we take care of the Americano soldiers. We know they came this way."

The prisoners locked in the smokehouse were calling for help. Peter was yelling the loudest of all. "Get us out of here!" he shouted. "The crazy Americano lieutenant has taken my mother and gone up to the canyons with her."

"So?" said Padilla with interest, though he made no move to unlock the cell. "How many men did he have with him?"

"No more than six or seven," Peter replied. "Let me out—I must go help my mother."

"Is she pretty, your mother?" said Padilla with a leer. "Don't worry, boy, I will help her myself."

CHAPTER 16

Padilla led the charge through the arroyo that led up toward the Santa Ynez mountains. The hill rose abruptly, much steeper, and the bandit leader knew they must be gaining on the Americanos. Just past a line of live oaks, the gang broke into the open of a hillside covered in dry brownish grass and brush that reached to the horses' bellies.

Above them the long slope was mostly bare of trees, except for a grove of oaks about halfway up. The last two in a line of blue-clad forms could just be seen disappearing into the shadows under the trees. "We have them!" Padilla exulted. He waved the Colt rifle in an overhead arc. "At them, amigos!" he shouted.

But even mounted as they were, the incline of the hillside and the thick brush made the uphill attack slow work. Before the bandits had closed even half the distance to the trees, shots began to ring out from the Americanos' position.

Four Fingers heard a slug whistle past his ear, and another maldito took a bullet in his thigh. Padilla was still urging his men onward when the rifle fire seemed to converge on him. In quick succession one slug cut his reins, striking the roan in the neck, a second went through his hat, and a third struck the horn of the saddle. He wheeled and sawed the useless reins as the horse gave a terrified scream and toppled over down the slope.

Kicking his feet free of the stirrups as the roan fell thrashing to the ground, Padilla leaped clear, keeping the rifle uppermost as he landed. Lying in a prone position, he returned the gunfire, getting off three quick shots before sliding off down the hill to rejoin his men.

"Now what, Capitan?" Four Fingers wanted to know. "The gringos have the advantage of us. Why don't we leave them, the cowardly pigs, and return to more important business?"

"No!" Padilla insisted. "Do you want it said that we could not take care of a pack of Americano curs?"

"I do not care what someone says to me if he is willing to take my place and be shot at. Ayee! That one bullet burned my ear, it came so close!"

"That's it!" Padilla exclaimed. He felt the breeze that blew up the hill from the sea. "Perfect," he said.

"What are you saying?"

"Give me your piedras de lumbre, the flint-and-steel," Padilla demanded. "We'll burn them out!"

————

The wave of riders that swept around the Reed hacienda completely encircled the house. Paco cautioned Peter to make no noise that would give away their presence until it was known who these men were. Still shackled, Peter wrenched around and pressed his face against the narrow crack in the boards of the smokehouse door and tried to make out the identity of the newcomers.

It was confusing. Some were dressed like the boy's neighbors and relatives in Santa Barbara, but just as

Peter prepared to call out to them, a wild and fierce-looking American came into view. Paco and Luis jostled the boy as all tried to peer through the cracks. Peter angrily ordered them to stand aside!

One ruffian with his arm bound in a dirty bandanna and with the hems of his clothing trailing buckskin fringe jumped off his horse amid the crowd. The man vaulted the steps to the back porch of the house three at a time. Peter was about to yell a protest, then checked himself and gasped: This backwoodsman was riding Flotada!

Then Peter heard a familiar voice yelling, "Francesca! Francesca, where are you?"

"Father!" he called, pounding on the wall of the smokehouse. "Father, over here!" But his cries went unheard. Amid the din and chaos of the milling horses, no one could hear the boy's shout.

Frustrated, Peter watched through the crack as his father conferred with another man dressed in frontier leather. Will gestured angrily at the ground torn up by the pawing horses, then pointed up and down the coast. It took no words for Peter to understand the anguish that the muddled trail caused the man who was desperate to locate Francesca!

"Father!" Peter shouted again. Exhausted, he sank back against the wall. No one was coming; they were all about to ride away without ever knowing that he was there. "Father," Peter said once more, his voice barely above a whisper, "help me."

Suddenly the noise outside the smokehouse subsided. At first Peter thought his father and the other men had left; then he heard the sound of footsteps coming across the hard-packed earth directly toward Peter's prison.

Peter held his breath. With a roar and a deafening clang, a single shot took the lock off the smokehouse door.

When the dust cleared, Peter saw his father standing in the doorway, silhouetted against the bright light outside.

———

Leaving Sinnickson to bring the rest of the troop of riders, Will mounted Flotada with Peter on behind. Over his shoulder Will called out, "I can get ahead of them, head them off." Even with the double burden, the mighty gray horse sprang away from the trail and up a steep ridgeline, leaving behind all the others except one. At his side, stride for stride, galloped Tor Fowler on the buckskin.

The wind of their passage whipped away words like the spray over the prow of a ship under full sail. Peter dug his fingers into his father's shoulder and pointed toward a thick, black column of smoke rising from the arroyo that snaked upward toward the heights. Will nodded sharply, and Flotada instantly caught the clashing fears of both his riders. *What if they were too late?* The Barileno steed, in whom the blood of his Andalusian forebears still ran true, redoubled his efforts and thundered up the mountainside.

———

The first wispy tendrils of drifting smoke reached Francesca's nose before Falls had recognized the threat. He was still posturing in front of his men and bragging.

"The Mexicans have no stomach for fighting. Pretty soon Mitchell and the rest of our boys will venture out from town and we'll catch these bandits between us."

It had taken only a moment for the thick dry underbrush to catch fire. Then a heap of chaparral blazed up with an explosion like a bucket of coal oil thrown onto a blacksmith's forge, and the flames raced up the hill.

"We've got to get out of here!" said the marine named Hollis. "Quick!"

Still Falls hesitated.

"Come on, Lieutenant! We can't stay here!"

"Wait," said Falls. "I've got to think. If we go out of the cover of the trees, they'll ride us down."

"No time for thinking, sir. If we stay here, we'll be cooked alive like roosting pigeons."

"Wait," demanded Falls again. "Don't they know they're endangering the woman's life? Don't they care?"

"They are *bandits*, like the boy José tried to tell you," Francesca hissed. "Now let me go while there is still time." She gestured up the hill. "There is a place of bare rock. We can find safety if we hurry."

A thick cloud of brownish-gray smoke began to roll through the grove of trees. "We got to go, Lieutenant," said Hollis again, and took Francesca's arm. "C'mon, ma'am," he urged. "You show us the way, and I'll help you up."

"No!" Falls snarled. "She's my prisoner. It's a trick to get us killed; don't you see, a trick!"

Hollis ignored him and started up the slope with Francesca. A heavier wall of dense smoke poured across the hillside like a wave of dirty seawater.

Falls snapped back the hammer on his carbine and fired at Hollis. Beside her, Francesca felt Hollis's grip tighten suddenly and then fall away. "Go on," he choked. "He's crazy." The marine slumped to the ground.

Francesca ran through the trees, reaching the clear hillside at the top of the grove. The sound of gunfire, mingled with the roar of the inferno on the hillside below, swept toward her. She blundered into a gully, gagging and coughing from the smoke and struggling to fight her way clear of the brush.

A swirl of wind parted the column of fumes overhead. In that instant Francesca could see the barren pinnacle of rock that was her goal, and she corrected her course toward it. Another bramble-choked gully appeared across her path and Francesca hesitated, not sure whether to force a way across or look for a way around.

In that moment's hesitation came a noise from behind her. Out of the wall of smoke stumbled Falls, his face a mask of soot and dried blood, his clothing torn. He had lost his rifle. His eyes had a frantic light, like a rabid wolf, a demonic figure come to life from the painted panels in the mission church.

Spirals of flame lit up the pall of smoke behind him. Incoherent ravings rumbled from his mouth, and he prepared to spring toward Francesca.

Francesca raised her arms to ward off the leap of the American lieutenant. In the next instant she felt her arms surrounded and pinned to her sides.

But it was not Falls's loathsome embrace that grasped her around the middle—it was the expertly cast reata of her son, who stood on the pinnacle of safety above her head. "Hold tight, Mother," Peter called.

Beside her son was her husband, pulling her to safety with mighty yanks of his strong left arm. "Hang on, Francesca," he urged. "We've got you."

Francesca felt herself being lifted and swung over the gully, away from Falls and away from the flames. Looking up in amazement, she saw Will, her son, and a third man she did not know, reeling her upward with mighty pulls that raised her a yard at a time.

Falls made a futile jump after Francesca that sent him sprawling into the midst of the brambles. He floundered for a moment before pulling himself, torn and bleeding, to the other side.

Emerging from the chaparral without an instant to spare as the flames raced up the gully, Falls began to climb the rock face. Behind him the heat of a thousand furnaces charred the back of his uniform and singed the hair on his head.

The lieutenant was halfway up the stone strata when another figure appeared behind the wall of flame. Padilla, fleeing from the forty horsemen who had caught him in his own trap, had hurriedly reloaded his rifle and was ascending the ridgeline right on the heels of the flames, in hopes of escaping the riders. He did not know Falls, but saw in the lieutenant's form someone who was standing in the way of his escape.

Padilla raised the Colt revolving rifle to his shoulder and fired. At first it seemed to have no effect on the climber, and Padilla wondered if he had somehow missed. He aimed and prepared to fire again, but stopped as Falls began to peel away from the rock face.

Little by little the American's hands and feet let go, and his body crumpled backward. He turned a somersault, and then his carcass crashed into the blazing brush of the arroyo.

Glancing around quickly, Padilla searched for a spot where the fast-moving flames were already dying down and he could cross to the other side. A bullet struck the ground near his feet. The shot had come from above! Throwing his head back in disbelief, Padilla saw Tor Fowler reloading a rifle on the knoll above him.

The cursed Americano! Padilla would finish him now, before the fool even had a chance to reload. He threw the Colt up to his shoulder, drew a bead on the front of Fowler's buckskin shirt, and pulled the trigger.

The hammer landed squarely, exploding the percussion cap. The powder of the cylinder under the hammer ignited with a roar . . . and so did the next cylinder, and the next and the next in uncontrolled chain firing. The frame and the barrel of the Colt disintegrated, taking Padilla's face and arms with them. With an unearthly scream, Padilla toppled forward and rolled into the inferno in the gully, stopping only when his corpse bumped against another body in the flames.

The shot intended for Tor Fowler hammered into the stock of the rifle, down near the ground. The weapon flew out of the mountain man's hands, but did not distract him from seeing Padilla's end. "I told Davis them rifles ain't safe," he muttered as he watched the two bodies disappear into the roaring flames. He shook his head. "Not even havin' company for the trip will help where them two is goin'."

EPILOGUE

Will regarded Tor Fowler on the prancing buckskin horse. "You're a good man, Fowler," he said. "Why not give a pass to the rest of this war and stay here in Santa Barbara?"

Fowler shook his head. "I figger to clear my name with Captain, no, *Governor* Fremont," he corrected himself. " 'Sides, mebbe I can speak up for doin' right by you Californios."

"Why don't you ride with *us*?" Sinnickson asked Will. "The three of us together might convince both sides to leave off fighting."

"Sorry," Will said, his good arm around Francesca. Peter stood close beside him. "But do what you can. Enough innocent folks have been hurt already." He gestured toward the infant Limik, sleeping in Simona's arms. "When the shaking out is all over, come on back and we'll build something good. Vayan con Dios," he said. "Go with God."

If you would like to contact the authors,
you may write them at the following address:

Bodie and Brock Thoene
P.O. Box 542
Glenbrook, NV 89413